The Duke Trap

Determined Debutantes
Book 3

Bianca Blythe

© Copyright 2022 by Bianca Blythe
Text by Bianca Blythe
Cover by Wicked Smart Designs

Dragonblade Publishing, Inc. is an imprint of Kathryn Le Veque Novels, Inc.
P.O. Box 23
Moreno Valley, CA 92556
ceo@dragonbladepublishing.com

Produced in the United States of America

First Edition April 2022
Trade Paperback Edition

Reproduction of any kind except where it pertains to short quotes in relation to advertising or promotion is strictly prohibited.

All Rights Reserved.

The characters and events portrayed in this book are fictitious. Any similarity to real persons, living or dead, is purely coincidental and not intended by the author.

ARE YOU SIGNED UP FOR DRAGONBLADE'S BLOG?

You'll get the latest news and information on exclusive giveaways, exclusive excerpts, coming releases, sales, free books, cover reveals and more.

Check out our complete list of authors, too!

No spam, no junk. That's a promise!

Sign Up Here

www.dragonbladepublishing.com

―――※―――

Dearest Reader;

Thank you for your support of a small press. At Dragonblade Publishing, we strive to bring you the highest quality Historical Romance from some of the best authors in the business. Without your support, there is no 'us', so we sincerely hope you adore these stories and find some new favorite authors along the way.

Happy Reading!

CEO, Dragonblade Publishing

Additional Dragonblade books by Author Bianca Blythe

Determined Debutantes Series
The Secret Life of a Debutante (Book 1)
You've Got an Earl (Book 2)
The Duke Trap (Book 3)

The Duke Trap

Leonora Holt never expected that her two younger sisters would find love before her. Lately she's grown disconcertingly accustomed to her brother's sighs and hints that she needs to marry. How can she find anyone when one dreadful man, the Duke of Dartmouth, is intent on reminding all the *ton* of her mother's scandal?

Sebastian, the Duke of Dartmouth, knows he should probably forget how the Holt family destroyed the last years of his father's life. At one point, he even considered Leonora Holt his best friend. Of course, that was when he was ten, and he's achieved far more wisdom since then. He's also gained a secret, but that's something he has no intention of ever revealing.

Leonora is determined to trap Sebastian. If his reputation is maligned, perhaps he will halt disparaging her family. Fortunately, she has the perfect plan, one that absolutely does not involve falling in love with the duke herself.

Chapter One

The bishop spoke, the guests prepared to applaud, and Leonora Holt tried to pretend that Sebastian, the Duke of Dartmouth, was not sitting in the third pew.

Unfortunately, pretending was impossible, even from her vantage point beside her sister and minister. It would be easier if the duke weren't so tall, and if his shoulders weren't quite so wide. It would also be easier if he weren't so handsome. His tousled hair glinted under the sunlight streaming through the stained glass windows, and his cravat looped in an interesting manner beneath his sturdy jaw.

Her eyes met his, and Sebastian raised an eyebrow nonchalantly. His perfect, succulent lips formed a smirk, and she frowned. Clearly, she'd trained her eyes to have too high a regard for symmetry and ideal forms.

Sebastian's emerald eyes shimmered, the color made brighter by his dark-umber hair. His skin was pale: no doubt the man spent time ruminating on how he might harm people, inside his various castles and elaborate town houses rather than enjoying the fresh air like most people.

The bishop was speaking, and Leonora forced her gaze away from the duke. Her sister was getting married. That was far more important.

Leonora had known Cornelius since she'd been young,

though she'd never imagined there might be a romance between Eloisa and him. She glanced at her older brother. His expression remained stern, and Leonora sighed. She'd thought Timothy would be pleased to realize his best friend would always be a part of their family life. In fact, she'd thought he'd overcome his initial shock.

Leonora followed Timothy's gaze, then her expression sobered. He was looking at a woman: Mama.

Leonora swallowed hard. No wonder Timothy's expression had been somber.

Normally Leonora might have been pleased when her mother was present, but that had been *before*.

Before Mama had decided to pose nude for the painter Julius's latest collection.

Before Mama had caused a scandal throughout the *ton*.

The other members of the audience gazed nervously at Mama as if she might decide to undress right there and then.

Mama, though, was clothed in an immaculate peach dress and a large stovepipe bonnet. Even the expansive brim and the crown trimmed with ostrich feathers couldn't obscure her wide smile and gleeful expression.

Finally, Cornelius and Eloisa exchanged vows, and the guests clapped. Cornelius and Eloisa strode down the aisle. The overlay of Eloisa's gown glimmered in the light, and Cornelius's beam was impossibly broad.

A nervous-looking organist pounded on the keys, and everyone tossed rice from their reticules.

Leonora followed the newly married couple, careful not to look in Sebastian's direction. Children cheered as they exited the church and flung flower petals. The sun had decided to radiate at full force, a rarity in April, and all the world smiled.

People surged around Eloisa and Cornelius, unperturbed by the portico's thick Corinthian columns, and offered their congratulations.

Cornelius's driver pulled up in Cornelius's barouche, and

Eloisa and Cornelius entered the elegant carriage. Someone had hung a wreath over the barouche, and the crowd exclaimed as the horses trotted away and led the couple to their new future together.

Leonora was happy for Eloisa.

Utterly happy.

Still, Leonora's heart ached. Things were now different. Leonora glanced at Sabrina, but she was joyfully clapping her hands beside her betrothed. Leonora felt guilty for her sudden melancholy.

"And now for the wedding breakfast," Timothy declared and marched in the direction of his town house.

Leonora wrapped her shawl more tightly to her, lest it flutter away with the breeze, and strolled after her brother. People thronged about her, chattering merrily about the loveliness of the wedding and Eloisa.

"Your younger sister got married before you," a velvety voice said.

Leonora turned, then scowled.

It was *him*.

Sebastian stood beside her. Worse, he was smirking.

Leonora forced her features to remain placid. "I didn't think you would be here, Your Grace."

He gave her a wry smile, and his dark eyebrows, the same color as his glossy coiffure, moved downward. "I'm at every event, Miss Holt."

"I thought you despised our family. Has that changed?" Leonora adopted her most saccharine tone.

"Naturally not."

They strode in unison toward her brother's house. She suddenly wished Timothy's house were far closer. If only someone could rescue her from the duke. The man's masculine scent was distracting.

"Oh, darling!" An alto voice Leonora could never forget interrupted her thoughts. "How lovely to see you!"

"Good morning, Mama." Leonora shot her mother a wobbly smile.

Personally, Leonora would have found it lovelier if Mama had decided not to come to the wedding. Everyone was looking at her curiously. Even if they hadn't seen the painting at Lady Richmond's town house, all the scandal sheets had written about it.

Everyone knew Mama had posed for a nude painting, and even though the painter in question, Julius, was famous and frequently won awards when his paintings weren't being banned, all the *ton* had been scandalized.

Leonora and her sisters hadn't thought they would be able to marry, but somehow, Eloisa had managed to win the viscount's heart, even though everyone knew one wasn't supposed to fall in love with one's older brother's best friend. Even Leonora's youngest sister, Sabrina, had found love with an earl whom she'd long admired.

Now Leonora was officially allowed to continue her season. Leonora doubted she would get a second one, and if any scandal occurred, Timothy might decide it was better to send her off to be a companion or governess to someone after all. His main concern was the reputation of his wife and unborn children.

"You appear glum." Mama took Leonora's arm and wrapped it tightly with her own, ignoring the duke's presence beside them. Mama's familiar scent of roses and musk wafted over Leonora. "Don't worry. You'll marry too."

A few people turned toward them, their eyebrows perched at unusually high positions.

"Mama!" Leonora said, and her cheeks warmed. She didn't want anyone to think she was concerned about finding a husband. Sebastian's comments had been sufficiently infuriating.

"I know how hard it is for you," Mama continued, "since you are the oldest child. No doubt you did not anticipate that your younger sisters would find love before you. You will marry though."

"I-I know."

Leonora wished Mama's voice did not carry with so much force. If only Mama hadn't mastered elocution. She'd been on the stage before Papa had married her, and clearly, speaking loudly was the sort of thing one never forgot.

Leonora cast a nervous glance around and caught Sebastian's eyes. His lips were curled in blatant amusement. She looked away abruptly. She was not going to focus on him. It didn't matter what he thought—he already despised her.

Still, she would rather he wouldn't feel sorry for her.

"You truly are pretty," Mama said, evidently taking Leonora's horrified expression as a sign of doubt and not outrage at the inappropriateness of the conversation. "A bit tall, of course. And you don't have your sister Sabrina's bosom or bottom."

"Mama!" Leonora exclaimed sternly.

"Still, surely, *someone* will marry you."

Tittering sounded around them, and when Leonora looked about her, some women were clutching their lace-embroidered handkerchiefs to their mouths and others were pondering the facade of St. George's with rather more intensity than the task demanded. Timothy had invited a large crowd, as if to prove the family was no longer tainted by scandal.

"Perhaps we can speak about something else," Leonora said miserably.

"But marriage should be possible," Mama insisted.

"That's not a concern," Leonora said softly.

"Your brother seems to think so," Mama said.

Leonora jerked her head toward her mother. "Indeed?"

"Indeed." Mama gave a contented smile, the sort people were prone to displaying when they had some gossip their conversation partners had not yet obtained.

Leonora gave an exasperated sigh. "You shouldn't have been invited," she said finally.

Mama widened her eyes. "You don't mean that."

"I do. You disappeared. I haven't seen you in ages. And now, during my season, you appear when you're at your most scandalous."

"Are you telling me I am interrupting your marital plans?" Mama asked.

Leonora wrinkled her brow, then bit her lip. "No," she admitted. "That's not quite true."

"I know," Mama said. "Timothy said there wasn't a single man you expressed any interest in. He's even contacted the woman who ran your finishing school. What was her name?"

"Mrs. Feldman, Mama," Leonora said. "Her name is in the finishing school name. You would know it if you'd paid the least bit of attention over the years."

"Oh." Mama blinked and had the good sense to look guilty.

Leonora sighed and quickened her pace. Her shift was suddenly far too tight. She must speak to her maid about that. She marched over the pink-and-white buds scattered over the pavement and didn't pause to inhale the fragrant scent of the blossoming trees about her. Normally, when she took walks with her sisters, she might pause to exclaim over the magnificent facades on some of the town houses, determining which half-naked Grecian god or goddess the architect had chosen to adorn the house with, and musing over the appropriate ferocity of the cast-iron door knockers, shaped like bears and lions.

She glanced at Sabrina, who was strolling slowly with the Earl of Plymouth. On occasion, her sister threw her head back and laughed. The earl's gaze was besotted.

Her mother was correct. She did need to find a husband of her own. Unfortunately, the task didn't fill her with enthusiasm.

Chapter Two

WEDDING GUESTS THRONGED the foyer, obscuring the coquelicot wallpaper Constance had recently installed. The servants had rearranged the furniture, no doubt to make the best use of the space.

Leonora sauntered toward her sister, past the floral and musk concoctions wafting through the narrow room. "Congratulations. I am so very happy for you."

Eloisa offered her an angelic smile. "Thank you."

In the next moment, Eloisa was swept away by the other guests, who hugged and embraced her.

"Time to eat!" Timothy announced gleefully, rubbing his hands. Evidently her brother had seen cook's delicacies.

Everyone filed into the dining room. Vibrant, colored punch glimmered from crystal tumblers, and delicious lamb and bread scents inundated Leonora's nostrils.

The guests sat to indulge in the delicious wedding breakfast that cook had spread before them and glanced at the wedding gifts piled around the fireplace. The wooden mantel seemed in danger of toppling from the considerable presents, and a large, rectangular gift Leonora did not recognize leaned against the wall.

"You must open your presents, Eloisa!" Sabrina clapped her hands and gestured to the various wrapped gifts about them.

The others concurred.

Sabrina pointed to the rectangular gift that towered even over the sizable mantel. "I'm quite curious about that one."

"Very well." Eloisa strode toward it. "Join me, Cornelius."

Her new husband rose obediently. His gaze remained fixed on Eloisa, as if she was a beautiful sculpture he could not believe was not only real but also his wife.

Leonora ignored the sudden pang that came through her at the sight of his obvious adoration for her younger sister. What might it be like to be so in love? Even her younger sister, Sabrina, was betrothed.

She turned her attention to the stack of gifts. Some of the items she recognized, but what was in that large, rectangular package? It almost resembled a painting. She frowned. Surely it wouldn't be a painting.

Though Leonora had always thought of herself as more of an art enthusiast than not, lately she'd grown weary of paintings. After all, Mama had posed for Julius for some particularly scandalous ones that had found their way through London's high society. Leonora could only imagine what would happen if Eloisa unwrapped such a painting before the various guests, and her stomach contracted.

Leonora glanced at the various aristocrats. How many were here simply for curiosity? Would they be sympathetic if Eloisa unwrapped a scandalous painting? Or would they be appalled that they'd taken a chance on the family and be eager to gossip to the rest of the *ton*?

Leonora bit her lip and glanced at Julius. "You didn't by any chance gift Eloisa a painting?"

A pained look appeared on Julius's face, and he raised his chin. "My paintings are the pinnacle of art. Indeed, one could say that all previous art methods have led up to my particular painting style. Would I ever gift a piece to someone who, for some utterly absurd reason, does not appreciate it?"

"I don't know," Leonora admitted. "Is that rhetorical?"

Julius rolled his eyes and banged a fist on the table, and some of the silver cutlery clinked together. "No! Of course not. My paintings deserve to be adored. They should be lauded and extolled. Not tolerated and certainly not banished to an attic or, worse yet, a cellar."

Leonora's shoulders eased. No doubt it was quite a normal painting. The label must simply have fallen off. Perhaps it was not even a painting at all.

Eloisa grinned, marched to the present, undid the red ribbon, and removed the cheesecloth wrapping.

A gilt-framed painting sparkled under the sunlight that streamed into the room.

There was silence.

Eloisa blinked furiously, and her husband's face was tight and withdrawn.

The painting was unmistakable.

Mama was splayed over the canvas. Her red hair, so like Leonora's and her sisters', cascaded down her shoulders. Heavens, that alone would be scandalous. Hair was supposed to be worn in chignons or tucked underneath bonnets or turbans. Hair was not supposed to cascade down shoulders.

But far worse than the hair, which seemed to serve as a beacon, was the rest of the painting.

Mama was nude.

Again.

Rounded breasts were fully visible, as were the hard rosy peaks. Mama's similarly rounded hips were hardly less scandalous. Red pubic hair curled over the place where Mama's legs joined, and Leonora looked away.

Timothy marched toward the painting. His footsteps clunked against the wooden floorboards.

No one spoke, even though a moment ago the whole room had been filled with celebratory noises.

Timothy turned the painting over, as if the dull brown back could possibly make anyone forget the scandalous, vibrant picture they'd just seen. He glared at Julius. "Is this your idea of a jest?"

Julius's eyebrows leaped up with the speed of an athlete. "You needn't be so horrified. Your sister has received great art."

"This painting is indecent. Vile. Appalling. Despicable," Timothy blustered, and his face turned an odd purple shade.

"No one insults my paintings!" Julius sprang from his seat and barreled toward Timothy. His tailcoats flapped behind him as he slid over the newly polished floor.

"Julius!" Mama called after him, but her voice was drowned by the flurry of sounds around her.

Timothy and Julius ran into the next room, trampling over the carpets with the vigor of vintners stomping over grapes.

Footmen pressed themselves against the wall, clutching the silver platters of breakfast food with two hands instead of their customary one.

Eloisa's eyes took on a dewy quality, and the rapidity of her blinks soared.

Oh no.

Eloisa shouldn't be upset. This was her wedding. This was supposed to be the happiest day of her life. Leonora glanced around the room at the horrified expressions on the guests. Some dropped their mouths open, others raised their eyebrows, and still others paled and gripped hold of the arms of their chairs, as if to assure themselves that life had not utterly ended.

One guest, though, didn't have a horrified expression on his face.

Sebastian.

His countenance was calm, and his emerald eyes danced. Though his lips weren't precisely drawn into a smirk, they didn't tremble and they weren't withdrawn.

Steel entered Leonora's spine. This was Sebastian's doing.

Leonora was certain of it.

Even Julius would have known better than to try to gift a painting of Mama at Eloisa's wedding, and he certainly wouldn't have denied it.

Timothy continued to chase Julius about the house, but no one was paying attention to Sebastian. Leonora's fists tightened. At one point, when she had still measured her age in single digits, she would have considered Sebastian her best friend. How things had changed.

"You did this," she said to Sebastian. Her voice wobbled uncharacteristically, but the man only smiled.

Heavens. This brought him amusement?

Timothy's eyebrows darted up. Constance's mouth dropped, then she shook her head at Leonora. Even her sisters appeared baffled.

Leonora's shoulders drooped. She'd just accused a duke of doing something terrible, and nobody believed her. Why should they? He was a duke, and she was the unmarried oldest daughter of a scandalous widow.

Now was not the time for accusations. Now was the time for rescuing her sister's wedding.

Leonora rose and forced a bright smile onto her face. "Who would like to listen to some music?"

The guests eagerly expressed their interest.

Leonora moved to the drawing room, thankful when the guests followed her. She sat at the piano. The glossy black-and-white keys gleamed in their familiar manner, and her breath no longer surged unnaturally. She put her fingers on the keys and played the quickest, happiest song she could remember. Soon the guests were singing to the music.

Cornelius shot her a grateful smile, but Leonora's mind remained on what had happened.

>>>>❀<<<<

SEBASTIAN MARCHED FROM the wedding. All his senses were alight. Happiness drifted through him. The birds seemed to be chirping with extra enthusiasm. This was an excellent day. His plan had worked perfectly. It would have been even more improved if Leonora had not distracted everyone by playing the piano. Blast, she'd even played it very well. Sebastian had not waited to hear just how many pieces she could perform.

When Sebastian had been little, Timothy had hidden frogs in Sebastian's lunch pail, even though Timothy had been *certain* Sebastian would scream and the others would laugh. Thankfully, Sebastian was now a duke, and people hardly ever laughed at him. Now *they* were frightened.

Even the sky had decided to turn a joyful shade of blue instead of its customary and dignified gray, as if it were pretending to be in one of those Italian Renaissance paintings filled with half-naked gods and goddesses prancing from cloud to cloud.

Sebastian turned toward Covent Garden, careful as always to make certain no one was following him. Life was very good indeed.

CHAPTER THREE

*T*HAT WRETCHED MAN. *That wretched, horrid man.*

Leonora's fingers shook as she entered the empty drawing room. She settled onto the piano bench. The teal armchairs and sofa were empty, their gilded legs sparkling, as if enjoying not being hidden by anyone's afternoon dress or trousers. Leonora flung her fingers over the keys of the piano. Unfortunately, Mozart's best efforts at composition could not distract her from that abominable man.

Heavens, Sebastian had seemed so pleasant when he was little. Leonora wouldn't make the mistake of poor judgment anymore. Something had to be done. Eloisa's wedding had almost been entirely ruined, and Sabrina was getting married next. Who knew how Sebastian might decide to embarrass the family?

No, he needed to be stopped.

He needed to be embarrassed.

The only problem was that there was not much about the duke that was embarrassment-worthy. Not his dark eyes, and not his exquisitely tousled hair. Each strand remained in a perfect place. The man's clothes were always tailored, displaying his broad shoulders and long, ever so long, legs.

Despite herself, Leonora swallowed.

No, Sebastian wasn't going to be an embarrassment on his

own.

Perhaps, just perhaps, she could assist. After all, Sebastian was a man, and every woman knew men could be trapped.

Leonora halted her music playing suddenly and glanced at one of the large broadsheets piled on the mahogany-and-walnut inlaid table. Normally her brother read a broadsheet while Leonora, her sisters, and Constance sewed. Timothy would comment about the various happenings in London and the wider world, no doubt only sharing the news he deemed appropriate for their ears.

He never spoke about the theater, but this was London, the largest city in the world. Surely a broadsheet would mention plays. And if there were plays, there were actresses. And if there were actresses... Leonora grinned. Well, then she could trap Sebastian.

Leonora rose from the piano bench. She softened her steps, lest Timothy wonder why she suddenly desired to read the broadsheet herself, then reached for it.

The paper was rough against her fingers, and it was still warm from the butler's ironing. Timothy wasn't a proponent of having inky fingers. He also wasn't a proponent of reading a creased broadsheet, and Leonora opened the pages carefully, jumping at the rustling sound that the thin pages produced. She moved quickly through the paper, noting various headlines about murders in the London docks and battles on the continent.

Finally, she came to the theater section. *Wonderful.*

Leonora removed the theater page carefully from the broadsheet, folded the paper, then tiptoed toward her room. Her heart raced.

"Leonora," Timothy boomed, and Leonora jumped up.

Heavens, her brother had caught her removing a section of the broadsheet.

She turned her head toward Timothy's surprised face. His pale-blue eyes seemed even larger than normal, and his equally pale, red brows had evidently decided that now was a good time to explore venturing up his vast forehead.

"I'm sorry." Leonora stood awkwardly in the living room. She shifted her weight from one leg to the other, as if somehow that could lessen the mortification surging through her. The whole point of this was not that she would be mortified; it was so Sebastian would be mortified. So far, the plan was not proceeding well. She forced a smile upon her face. "I would like to see a play," Leonora said.

"A play?"

"Indeed."

"Oh." Timothy frowned slightly, though his eyebrows were no longer at their former lofty position.

"Or an opera," Leonora stated.

"I'm not certain either is a respectable place for a young woman."

"But surely if our whole family goes…"

Timothy sighed. "Very well. I suppose we could do that." He tilted his head. "Is there anything in particular you want to see?"

Leonora smiled and pointed to an opera on the broadsheet. "This would do quite well."

"All right. As you desire."

She finally closed the door and went to her desk, where she removed some paper and a quill.

"You're smiling."

Leonora stiffened immediately and jerked her head toward her sister's voice.

Sabrina's eyes rounded. "Did I startle you? I'm sorry, I—"

"No," Leonora squeaked. "I'm fine. Everything is fine."

She smiled.

For the first time since they'd arrived in London, Leonora knew this was true. She was going to ruin the duke's reputation. The whole town would know what kind of an awful, terrible man he truly was. Leonora had some pin money, and she was going to use all of it to pay for an actress.

Of course, it wasn't the sort of thing she could just about go around telling Sabrina. She was so happy and might try to dissuade Leonora from her plan. Instead, Leonora pasted a smile upon her face. "I simply didn't hear you."

"Oh." Sabrina nodded. She glanced around. "It is strange not having Eloisa here, isn't it?"

Normally Leonora would always hear chatter around her, but now things were different. Soon things would be even more different.

"You're getting married as well," Leonora reminded her.

"Yes," Sabrina said, and her cheeks pinkened so prettily that Leonora's heart ached.

Leonora wanted Sabrina to have the very best wedding. Once she found someone to help her lay a duke trap, everything would be perfect. Leonora knew just whom she would ask.

⁂

A THRILL OF pleasure moved through Leonora as she entered Covent Garden. She was accustomed to playing the piano for her friends and family, but as much as she adored music, she'd never attended an opera before. Excitement thrummed through her, even though she was here not entirely for pleasure and even though the opera was famous and she already knew the plot.

The female lead's character was suffering from a terrible illness and would not reappear until the next act. This was the time to attempt to speak with the opera's star. She eyed the red velvet curtains that led from her family's box, then glanced back at Timothy and Constance. Fortunately, their attention remained fixed on the stage.

Leonora disappeared through the curtain and entered the now empty corridor. She moved in the direction of the stage.

Everything was swathed in brilliant burgundies. Candles flickered from gold sconces, from which crystals dangled. It was the music, that lovely piano music, that most made Leonora's heart thrum. She'd insisted on attending for practical purposes. She'd never expected to find it so appealing. Timothy and Constance normally spoke about the opera in derogatory tones, declaring it melodrama for continentals.

The corridors were almost empty, a stark contrast to the bustle that had been present when they'd entered. This was the sort of conversation that was best not put on paper. Her coins jangled in her reticule, and she hurried backstage. Though some people gave her odd looks, none of them questioned her. Perhaps they assumed that a woman dressed as nicely as she was must be present for a reason.

Finally, Leonora found Mimi's dressing room and entered.

A beautiful woman sitting on a jonquil velvet chaise longue widened her large blue eyes. Her blonde hair was artfully arranged into ringlets, and her cheeks were such a vibrant pink Leonora wondered whether she was wearing French powder. The woman raised an elegant gloved hand toward her neck. "You're in my dressing room."

"I would like to hire you," Leonora blurted.

Mimi's immaculately formed eyebrows rose, then she smiled. "For a house party play. I understand." She leaned toward Leonora conspiratorially. "All your friends will be most envious of your production."

Leonora gave a weak smile. "Actually, I prefer discretion. I hope your services can be used for more private matters."

"Oh." Mimi's face whitened. "You better sit."

Leonora glanced about the crowded room. Fur shrugs were draped over jewel-tufted armchairs, and golden silver-framed mirrors adorned each wall, as if Mimi thought it a travesty were she to have to bother to crane her neck to catch a glimpse of her perfect visage. Finally, Leonora settled rigidly into a lacquered black chair decorated with gold finishes.

"You saw the ad for an actress in the paper," Mimi said softly once the door was shut.

Leonora nodded.

"I shouldn't have placed it. I was irritated. I had been promised some work, then the client had the audacity to use someone else." Mimi's eyes flashed, and Leonora understood why she'd captivated London audiences.

No wonder she'd been hired to perform here. She would captivate anyone. She would certainly captivate Sebastian.

Leonora waited for a sense of pride to surge through her, but only a flicker of distaste came. No doubt that was out of some misguided sense of loyalty to the solemn-eyed boy with whom she'd used to play. That had been when Papa was still alive, before she knew of the vast, irrational hatred the people in the neighboring estate held for her family.

Leonora never would have considered her once dear friend would so throw himself into the task of being a duke that he would adopt every prejudicial opinion formed when witches were still being burned.

Certainly, Leonora was absolutely not feeling jealousy. That would be absurd. Even if she wished Mimi were not quite so enticing. The actress's flaxen hair was the sort men went mad for, as if they thought they were securing an actual angel.

"What is the assignment?" Mimi asked.

"I want to destroy a man." The words galloped from Leonora's throat.

"I don't murder," Mimi said. "I seduce."

"I know," she whispered, and her skin warmed.

"I wouldn't have thought a woman like you knew much about seduction," Mimi said dryly, and Leonora flushed.

She ran a hand against her hair, conscious the curls did not appear as soft and glossy as Mimi's. Her hair was too thick for such things. It was a wonder they'd been tamed into an updo at all. Her lady's maid constantly gritted her teeth when preparing Leonora's unstylishly red hair for balls and other events. No, she wasn't the sort that men adored.

"My friend is holding a ball. I'm going to secure you an invitation posing as a Lady Seneca Footwall. There's a man I want you to get in to an improper position."

Mimi raised her eyebrows. "Indeed?"

Leonora nodded solemnly. "Yes, but preferably publicly. And then I want you to be upset about it."

"I see," the actress said, her voice grave.

"I'll pay you handsomely."

"Are you certain you want to destroy a man's reputation like that?"

"He's a terrible man." Leonora ignored sudden twinges of something that seemed too similar to self-reproach. "People need to know. It's the only thing."

Chapter Four

Even though it was already evening, the sun was still at almost its normal force. Leonora clutched her reticule. She pushed away the slight guilt that she was here on her own. Mimi didn't live far from Hyde Park, and she'd been able to slip away from the others.

Sabrina and Percival were so busy looking into each other's eyes that when she'd murmured she noticed a friend in the park, they hadn't even turned to look.

What might it be like to be so in love?

Leonora checked her address for a third time, then gazed at the narrow dark brick town house. She shuddered, even though it was hardly very cold. This must be Mimi's residence.

Somehow, Leonora had imagined the town house would be more elegant. After all, in Covent Garden, Mimi had played a wealthy courtesan and had been swathed in fur and silk.

There was still time to change her mind and disappear. It wouldn't be the most honorable thing, but she had paid the opera singer already. Did she want to risk having her be at the ball?

Leonora hesitated, but of course, there was only one answer. She strode forward, grabbed hold of the door knocker, and rapped on the door. The door was rather less glossy than that of Timothy's town house. No fluffy-maned lion adorned it.

The door swung open, and Mimi peeked her face out.

"It's you?" she breathed.

Leonora nodded.

"I thought you might change your mind."

"Of course not."

Mimi opened the door, and Leonora decided not to tell her she very nearly had not come.

Leonora handed her the embossed letter. "Just show that to the butler."

"Very well." Mimi tilted her head, and her golden locks, not yet put up, spilled about her shoulders. "Who is the gentleman in question that you would like me to—?"

"It's best you don't know yet," Leonora said.

Mimi laughed. "You mean I might change my mind if I knew the person's identity?"

"Something like that," Leonora said.

The man was, after all, a duke. That alone might make Mimi skeptical. Still, the plan was perfect. Mimi would have time to leave and would never be found.

"Very well." Mimi straightened her shoulders. "I will make certain people find us in a compromising situation."

"Splendid." Leonora forced her lips into a wide smile, but her voice shook. "I will see you at the ball. Here is—er—your invitation. I told the hostess, Lady Richmond, that you are a Lady Seneca Footwall. You're from the north. After the—er—incident, just leave the ball as quickly as you can. Everyone will think you returned home to the countryside in horror, and you'll be the last person the duke will want to speak to."

"You thought of everything."

Leonora nodded, then exited the town house. She hurried over the cobbled street, keeping her face down, until she reached the park and its lush perimeter. Pensile blossoms swung languidly from sturdy trees. The festive pink color varied from the sober browns and grays she'd grown accustomed to, and passersby strode about with wide smiles pasted uncharacteristically to their faces.

Leonora adopted the slower gait favored by those strolling through Hyde Park, as if she'd simply wandered off from her family to admire some flowers from a closer angle. Then she joined her sister and the Earl of Plymouth.

"Ah! You're back. Did you have a nice stroll?" the earl asked absentmindedly, keeping his eyes on Sabrina's visage.

"Indeed. I—er—was just speaking with a friend," Leonora said.

Percival and her sister were silent. Murmurings sounded from the other passersby, and their feet crunched over the twigs on the dirt paths.

"Sabrina and I should dress for the ball," Leonora said.

"Naturally." Disappointment fluttered over the earl's face, even though Leonora knew the earl would see Sabrina at Lord and Lady Richmond's ball tonight.

The earl pressed his lips against Sabrina's hand and murmured something in a low tone. Then he sauntered over the dirt path toward his town house, ignoring the simpering looks of tittering debutantes who had not managed to land him.

Leonora smiled at her younger sister. "I'm so happy for you—"

Sabrina jerked her hands to her waist and glowered. "Where were you?"

Leonora's eyes widened. Normally her sisters weren't ferocious.

"I-I was seeing a friend," Leonora stammered.

"You were not."

"Nonsense, we were just—" Leonora pointed in the vague direction of the Serpentine.

"I saw you leave the park."

Leonora's shoulders slumped. *Drat.*

"You should be grateful I didn't say anything to Percival," Sabrina continued. "He feels quite protective about the whole family, and I wouldn't have been surprised if he'd bounded after you."

"Why didn't you tell him?"

Sabrina gave a nonchalant shrug. "I was certain you must have a reason."

"I-I just wanted some fresh air," Leonora lied.

The less her sister knew about the plan, the better. Sabrina understood many things, but Leonora doubted that knowledge extended to the Duke of Dartmouth. After all, Sabrina had been young when Leonora had spent her time playing with Sebastian and had considered him her best friend. She didn't understand the duke's capacity to betray.

Sabrina arched an eyebrow. "We are in a park. Are you saying the wind patterns were not ideal in this section?"

"No, no," Leonora said reluctantly. "You're correct. I was going somewhere important."

Sabrina's eyes glistened, and she leaned forward. "You mean to say you have a secret lover?"

Leonora's heart thumped oddly, and her jaw fell. Sabrina's eyes continued to sparkle.

Leonora hastily shook her head. "Of course not."

"Oh." Sabrina's shoulders sank, and her voice sounded almost disappointed.

Was that truly what Sabrina had been thinking? And she'd then decided to be discreet? Heavens, Sabrina should certainly have said something if she thought Leonora might enter a compromising position. After all, everyone knew that was the worst thing that could befall a woman.

Still… It occurred to Leonora that Sabrina and Percival were exceedingly close. She was certain they were closer than most unmarried couples were. In fact, they seemed more devoted than most married couples. She'd once wondered whether she'd actually heard them doing improper things.

"What are you doing?" Sabrina asked.

"I'm taking care of matters."

"What matters?"

Leonora sighed. She shouldn't tell Sabrina, and yet whom

else could she tell? She didn't want to keep the secret alone any longer.

"What do you have in mind?" Sabrina pressed.

"I want to ensure the Duke of Dartmouth no longer is given such ridiculous respect."

Sabrina blinked.

"He tried to destroy Eloisa's wedding," Leonora reminded Sabrina.

Sabrina shifted her legs. "That's not proven."

Leonora gave her sister a hard stare. "You know the difficulties Eloisa had with him earlier?"

"I know," Sabrina admitted.

"So you see, I must handle the matter," Leonora said briskly.

Sabrina narrowed her eyes. "What do you have planned?"

"Something good. Something that will make him stop." Even though Leonora had been nervous all day, even though she despised that Sabrina and she were discussing this particular thing, her lips curled. "You'll find out tonight, in fact."

"Please don't tell me you bought a weapon."

"Of course not," Leonora said. "I will only damage his reputation. No one gets hurt. He will simply become less powerful than he would be otherwise. That's all."

Sabrina nodded, though it was clear from her expression she remained uncertain.

"I'm the oldest sister," Leonora reminded her. "I know best."

"I'm not certain you do," Sabrina said.

"Then you'll find out you were wrong to doubt me."

They hurried back in silence to the town house.

⇶⇷

SEBASTIAN SURVEYED THE ballroom with his customary efficiency. Clusters of matchmaking mamas and proud papas stared at him, as if pondering whether to draw up their courage to approach him. Sebastian doubted the room had been this silent before he'd entered. He marched past wallflowers and widows, debutantes and dandies, toward his friends.

Then he halted.

Miss Leonora Holt stood beside Cornelius and Percival. His throat dried automatically. She was clothed in a red gown that did interesting things to her skin. Her cheeks seemed pinker than normal, and her red hair utterly vibrant.

For an embarrassing moment, his chest tightened, and he had the horrible impression he might have a strange look fluttering over his face. Certainly butterflies seemed to have made their way inside his chest, flapping their wings nonchalantly against his inner organs.

"Ah! Dartmouth!" Percival waved to him, and Leonora turned.

Normally, when she turned toward him, she scowled and glowered. Now a faint smile flickered over her face. He longed to know what was amusing.

"I thought you might not be here," Percival said.

"I wouldn't miss a ball," Sebastian said, even though that was precisely what he'd considered doing earlier.

Unease moved through him, as if this was his very first event in society.

Then, he'd been aware of his reduced financial circumstances. Being at a ball had been less about dancing and more about a chance to meet the important people with whom he could make lucrative deals.

Personally, Sebastian found it preferable to spend his nights scribbling music than to attend these sorts of events. He was uncomfortable with gossip, wondering how much people's eyes might sparkle and shine should they learn the extent of his father's calamitous deal.

Music had been his favorite method for relaxation, though one was hardly required to wear a top hat and tails to indulge in that pastime.

A footman lowed a platter of champagne, and Sebastian picked up a flute and grasped the cold glass. It was better to focus on the faint sizzle of bubbles than on Miss Leonora Holt. It would be too easy to stare at her too long.

"I hope you are enjoying the ball, Miss Holt." Sebastian gave a slight bow and pretended he was speaking to his most casual acquaintance.

"Indeed." Her eyes glinted, and she gazed about the room. "Excuse me. I have noticed a friend."

With that, Leonora strode away. Her bottom moved in an interesting manner, and his throat dried.

Sebastian took a hasty sip of champagne. The bubbles prickled his throat but failed to distract him from his discomfort.

A cough sounded.

"How is the club?" Percival asked.

Sebastian turned his head toward his friend. Cornelius and Percival were both smiling, and Sebastian had the decidedly unpleasant sensation this was the second time in a row Cornelius had asked him this question.

"Everything is fine," Sebastian said tersely.

In truth, Sebastian assumed everything was fine. Actually, he hadn't visited Robertson's Gentlemen's Club in a while. Ever since Percival had decided to spend his time strolling with Sabrina in Hyde Park and calling on her despicable family, he'd abandoned the practice of visiting the club, favoring reading his paper at home.

"Ah." Percival nodded.

Something had changed. The conversation was strained. Perhaps they suspected he'd been responsible for gifting the painting. Timothy had seemed convinced Julius was behind it, but his friends knew him well.

For the first time, Sebastian wondered whether gifting Cornelius and Eloisa that painting had been the correct thing to do.

He turned to Cornelius. He hadn't seen him since the wedding. "How is married life?"

A blissful smile danced upon Cornelius's lips, and his eyes took on a distinct dewy tone. *Mighty Poseidon*. He'd always considered Cornelius a serious man, yet now he half expected the viscount to begin reciting poetry.

"Marriage is the most wonderful thing in the world," Cornelius mused.

"Ah." Sebastian gazed at the viscount skeptically.

Unlike Percival, Sebastian had never been opposed to marriage. In fact, one day, it would be quite useful for him to marry. That was the way to procure heirs. Still, Sebastian was young enough not to feel compelled to scour the ballrooms, looking for suitable brides. He didn't have any doubt that various proud papas and matchmaking mamas would be all too happy to recite their offspring's talents.

"I'm in no hurry for that day to come," Sebastian muttered.

"Many prospects are present," Cornelius observed.

"I'm only here because it's dull to be in Robertson's club."

"Some men favor gaming houses."

Sebastian wrinkled his nose. "I'll never visit those."

Cornelius's eyes widened somewhat, and Sebastian wondered if he'd been too forceful in his denouncement of those much-lauded institutions. In fact, some people at Robertson's Gentleman's Club gambled, though they did it with less rigor than at the various gaming houses, dotted about the capital, that came equipped with music and encouraging glances from paid female companions.

Sebastian shuddered, conscious Cornelius was tilting his head and narrowing his eyes.

"I shouldn't complain," Sebastian said. "It's not so terrible here." He swung his gaze around the room, realizing as he said them that his words were a lie.

This *was* terrible. Utterly terrible. Two rows of wallflowers were scrunched beside the fireplace and gray-haired women. All of them stared.

"Lady Richmond fancies herself a matchmaker," Percival said.

"Perhaps you could ask her about any suitable prospects."

"I doubt she's the only matchmaker present," Cornelius said.

Percival nodded authoritatively. "Matchmaking is an occupation more and more women are joining. Something perhaps about being able to tell their friends they owe their whole lifetime of happiness to them."

"I doubt that's true if the institution in question is marriage," Sebastian said.

Cornelius cleared his throat. "I will remind you I am married. In fact, I urge you to consider the institution."

Sebastian raised an eyebrow. "Is it truly that wonderful?"

A beatific smile drifted over Cornelius's face once more. "Is the seaside wonderful? The sun? The very stars?"

Sebastian smiled despite himself. "I still have time."

"For children, perhaps," Cornelius agreed. "But why postpone the most magnificent part of life?"

Sebastian gave his friend a wobbly smile. Normally he might have teased Cornelius for his statement, but he had the odd impression in this case he might be wrong. It was an unfamiliar sensation, one Sebastian abhorred.

"There's Lord Richmond," Percival declared, thankfully changing the conversation from Sebastian's marital status.

The host waddled toward him with a wide beam on his face. At his side was a young lady in a shimmering gown. Something about her seemed familiar.

"I don't recognize her," Cornelius said.

"Undoubtedly one of Richmond's relatives." Percival sipped his brandy.

"Lord Richmond doesn't view his relatives with such enthusiasm," Cornelius observed.

Sebastian followed the viscount's gaze. The woman did look dashed familiar. In fact, he would have sworn...

He shook his head. The woman he knew didn't have dark-brown hair. But then, wigs were just the sort of thing this woman would know about.

He narrowed his eyes. What was Mimi doing at Lord Richmond's ball? And why was she in disguise?

"She's probably from the countryside," Sebastian said.

Whatever Mimi was doing, no doubt she didn't want her identity to be advertised, and he didn't want to explain why he was acquainted with her.

"She doesn't dress like someone from the countryside," Cornelius muttered.

"I say, she looks rather like—" Percival halted his words rapidly, and a ruddy color spread over his cheeks. Percival cleared his throat. "I should check on Sabrina."

"Good idea," Sebastian said, ignoring Cornelius's quizzical look as Percival scurried away.

Percival had met Mimi before, though Sebastian was certain the earl had never told Cornelius.

"Good evening, gentlemen," Lord Richmond said in a jaunty tone.

Everyone exchanged bows.

"This is Lady Seneca Footwall," the host said regally. "She's a most enchanting young lady."

Lord Richmond's gaze flicked toward the lady's bosom, and his tongue darted from his small mouth, as if he was preparing to inspect it with that particular appendage.

Sebastian moved into a perfunctory bow.

He *definitely* knew the woman before him, and though he agreed she was enchanting—most of London shared that decidedly uncontroversial opinion—she was not Miss Seneca Footwall. He doubted anyone with that preposterous name even existed.

"What an unexpected pleasure," he murmured.

Mimi's face whitened, and she turned her head toward Leonora Holt slightly. Leonora nodded.

Why was Leonora nodding? How would the eldest Holt sister possibly be acquainted with Mimi? Surely her mother hadn't decided to introduce her to actresses in addition to artists?

Sebastian's forehead wrinkled. This was dashed odd. Though he was all for having performers flood the *ton*'s favorite assembly rooms and ballrooms, he doubted Lord and Lady Richmond were similarly enthusiastic at that particular prospect.

"Your name is Lady Seneca Footwall?" Sebastian ventured.

Mimi nodded, but her face was pink.

"Are those the Cornwall Footwalls or the Hampshire Footwalls?" Sebastian asked.

Mimi stepped back, then inhaled. "The Northumberland Footwalls."

"Ah." Sebastian nodded. "I was not aware there were so many Footwalls."

"We are a large family," Mimi said, evidently gaining confidence.

"Evidently." Sebastian narrowed his eyes. "And to think you have no trace of a Northern accent!"

"My—er—governess was from London."

"She sounds like she was from the East End of London," Sebastian muttered.

Mimi shot him a horrified glance, then shook her head slightly.

Sebastian smirked. "Tell me, are you fond of music, Lady Seneca?"

Mimi shifted her legs. "Isn't everyone fond of music?"

"I thought you might want to sing something," Sebastian said.

"Oh, no." Mimi tightened her lips. "I would be far too shy."

Sebastian raised an eyebrow. He'd heard Mimi sing plenty of times in Covent Garden. She'd never been too shy then, but no doubt she had no urge to be recognized.

"What a curious comment, Dartmouth," Lord Richmond said. "People don't sing at balls. The string quartet would get irritated."

"You're quite right," Sebastian said smoothly.

"Though," Lord Richmond said amiably, glancing at Mimi's

cleavage as if it provided fortification, "if you would like to sing, I can arrange it. I am the host, after all."

"That's unnecessary," Mimi said hastily.

"Your beauty doesn't extend to your vocal cords? Well, nothing to be done about that." He leaned nearer. "My wife's a dreadful singer. So is my daughter. It's a common affliction."

A pained expression descended over Lord Richmond's visage, as if recalling uncomfortable music performances in too-small parlors equipped with too little liquid sustenance.

"Miss Leonora Holt is an excellent pianist," Cornelius said. "If you wanted to hear some music."

Sebastian scowled. He did not want to hear about Miss Leonora Holt's no doubt exaggerated accomplishments. Memories of her performance at the wedding fluttered into his mind. Even earlier memories also descended. She had been damned good. No doubt he wouldn't have been able to chat with Percival and Cornelius with such ease if she hadn't rescued the wedding. A ruined wedding was the sort of thing a man might hold against one.

"I'm sure the string quartet is capable of handling tonight's music," Sebastian said.

Mimi's shoulders eased. Cornelius and Lord Richmond eyed him with strange expressions on their faces. The room was too hot, and Sebastian placed a finger inside his collar to loosen his cravat.

"Perhaps you would care to dance with Lady Seneca?" Lord Richmond asked.

"I—" Sebastian stared at Mimi.

Mimi's eyes were firmly fixed to the floor, and a pink stain spread over her cheeks. Whatever had brought her to this ball, surely it had nothing to do with him.

"I'm not in the mood for dancing," Sebastian declared.

"Oh!" Lord Richmond blinked, then grinned. "But I am! Shall we, Lady Seneca?"

With that, Lord Richmond led Mimi away. Sebastian turned

to Leonora, but she hastily strode away and joined her sisters.

Odd.

Had she been watching him?

For some reason, something about the way the candlelight flickered against her auburn hair made his heart tighten. For a redhead's, Leonora's eyelashes were thick and dark, and when she flickered her long lashes down, he wondered what she was thinking. Then he remembered he didn't need to ponder what was in her mind: undoubtedly she was thinking appalling things about himself.

Chapter Five

Leonora pretended she was not focused solely on the exchange between Sebastian and Mimi. Not that there'd been much of an exchange. Sebastian had barely spoken to her. He hadn't even offered to dance with her, much less allowed himself to be led to the balcony as Mimi and Leonora had planned.

Nothing had happened. Mimi had attempted so hard, and Sebastian hadn't seemed the least taken with the actress. How was Mimi supposed to be discovered in a compromising position with Sebastian if he didn't even so much as dance with her?

"Who is that brunette?" Sabrina asked.

"Lady Seneca Footwall."

Sabrina was supposed to smile and perhaps even nod, but instead she simply furrowed her brow. Sabrina opened her mouth, then sighed. "I've never heard that name before."

"She's from the north," Leonora said vaguely.

"How did you meet her?"

"I-I forget," Leonora replied. Unfortunately, her statement did not lessen the sternness of her sister's gaze.

Leonora shifted her legs, suddenly conscious of the thinness of her slippers and the manner in which she could feel the floorboards. "There are many people in the *ton* you do not know."

Leonora stared as Sebastian danced with a woman who was not Lady Seneca Footwall. Even though the ballroom was filled with giggling debutantes and nervous-looking women on their second and third seasons, it was impossible not to notice him. His sturdy back was always upright, and his chin was always thrust over his impeccably tied cravat. Every move was elegant and perfectly timed to the rhythm of the violins.

Sabrina cleared her throat, and Leonora's cheeks heated. She withdrew her gaze from Sebastian quickly, though she had the distinct impression it was not quickly enough. Her heartbeat fluttered oddly, as if her heart had just realized she'd rather be looking at him than anything else.

Obviously, she was being strategic.

She didn't *truly* want to gaze at Sebastian.

He wasn't the only man in the room with symmetrical features. At least, he was probably not the only man in the room with symmetrical features. Leonora had never noticed other men, but that was undoubtedly because she preferred to postpone that particular pleasure until after everything was resolved with Sebastian. Hopefully he would slink away in shame to his country manor.

Something panged in her chest.

She wouldn't miss him. She absolutely wouldn't miss him.

Leonora gritted her teeth. One wasn't supposed to find people of such despicable characteristics appealing. What would have happened if Wellesley or Nelson had spent time contemplating the overall wonderfulness of the French?

Leonora shuddered despite herself.

Eloisa and Sabrina had formed attachments to respectable men: Cornelius and Percival. And yet energy thrummed through her in Sebastian's presence, as if he was setting her alight. He might as well have been the sun, even though she'd never thought a sun god would stomp around with just that sort of smirk and have just those sort of dark eyes that read one's soul.

"She had something to do with your plan, didn't she?" Sabrina asked.

"Excuse me?" Leonora removed her fan from her reticule and flapped it over her face, lest people could wonder at her conversation topic. Leonora wouldn't be surprised if Sebastian was an expert in lip reading. The man emanated competence and intelligence. It was one of the many irritating things about him.

"Lady Seneca Footwall." A wrinkle appeared on Sabrina's normally pristine brow. "What did you think I was discussing?"

"O-Of course," Leonora said hastily. "It's just—er—"

Sabrina raised her eyebrow.

"It's not something to discuss here," Leonora said finally.

"I knew it." Sabrina's eyes blazed. "You are planning something with her. Outrageous."

Leonora drew back. "You haven't always been the symbol of propriety."

"No," Sabrina admitted, "perhaps not. Still, that doesn't mean you need to abandon decorum."

"I'm certain I don't know what you mean. But besides, my plan hardly worked, did it?" There was a bitter edge to Leonora's voice she couldn't disguise.

Lady Seneca Footwall was still speaking with Lord Richmond.

"No matter," Leonora said in her brightest voice. "I shall fix it myself."

"What do you mean?" Sabrina asked.

"I had wanted Lady Seneca Footwall to prove he is a dreadful man with no character, but instead, I will have to show that to the world."

Sabrina's mouth dropped open.

"Excuse me," she told Sabrina, then marched toward Mimi. Soon Leonora was face-to-face with the actress.

Mimi glanced at Lord Richmond. "Thank you for this lovely conversation."

"You can leave," Leonora said once Lord Richmond departed.

"I'm sorry." Guilt moved across the actress's beautiful face.

"It's not your fault," Leonora said. "You couldn't be more beautiful."

Mimi bit her lip, as if she wanted to say more, then headed to the exit.

Every other man in the room turned their necks to watch the actress glide toward the door.

Leonora pressed her lips together.

Perhaps Sebastian could not be trapped by the actress, but Leonora had no doubts about the man's character. She gritted her teeth. She would have to do the task herself.

A faint nervousness thrummed through her, but she ignored it. She wasn't going to let anyone harm her family again, even if the man doing the harming was a duke.

She wove her way through the ballroom, striding over the polished wooden floor. Dancers bounced up and down. A few people glanced at her curiously, and some men looked like they were pondering gathering their courage to ask her to dance. Leonora quickened her steps.

She would need to find a husband, but she had no urge to make stilted conversations in gardens and ballrooms with various prospects. None of the men had captured her imagination here. Once she settled things with Sebastian, she would be able to focus on the wonders of the men in the *ton*.

The sooner she settled this, the sooner the rest of her life could begin. When people knew about the duke's dastardly nature, they would be more suspicious of any other accusations he might bring against her family.

Leonora marched through the ballroom, seeking Sebastian's handsome figure.

"Miss Holt!" A voice interrupted her quest, and Leonora halted.

She turned to see an elderly woman with gray hair whom she recognized at once.

"Mrs. Feldman!" Leonora exclaimed.

"Indeed. I'm surprised this is our first encounter in London,"

Mrs. Feldman said.

Leonora attempted a wobbly smile, but Mrs. Feldman's eyes softened.

"I know this has been a difficult season for you," Mrs. Feldman said. "It must be trying to see your two younger sisters with their young men. To think they both landed aristocrats."

"I'm happy for my sisters," Leonora said distractedly, still craning her neck to see Sebastian.

Suddenly, his dark hair flashed before her. He held his back so elegantly. No wonder Daphne was smiling with such enthusiasm at him.

"A quite understandable impulse," Mrs. Feldman said.

"Excuse me?" Leonora jerked her head toward Mrs. Feldman. Had Mrs. Feldman caught her staring at Sebastian?

Leonora hardly wanted to give the impression of a lovesick little girl, but she didn't want anyone to think her a lovesick little girl given to impossible fantasies with Dartmouth. Her skin heated, as if Mrs. Feldman had set her hair alight.

"I meant you are a good sister," Mrs. Feldman said with a strange look on her face.

Even though Mrs. Feldman had emphasized at her finishing school the importance of not furrowing one's brow, lest wrinkles form, and keeping one's face placid at all times, even when reading the more distressing sections of the broadsheets, a distinct line now creased her forehead. "What did you think I was referring to?"

"Nothing," Leonora said hastily. "Forgive me, I'm unaccustomed to being around such crowds."

Mrs. Feldman continued to assess her. "Perhaps I should consider adding taking my charges to crowded situations to the curricula. I thought it unnecessary, but—"

"Perhaps you could," Leonora said with as much enthusiasm as she could muster. Unfortunately, she had the horrible sensation she'd overcalculated and was now grinning at Mrs. Feldman in a quite unladylike manner.

"My dear, you are nervous," Mrs. Feldman said. "Deep breaths, sweetheart. Breaths are wondrous things." Mrs. Feldman leaned toward her, and her eyes sparkled uncharacteristically. "I have some good news. My nephew is at this ball, and he is looking for a bride. You and he could be most suited. With my recommendation, naturally. He values my opinion. He is an excellent nephew."

The music stopped. Was Sebastian going to dance with someone else now? Leonora couldn't allow that to happen. Dances stretched on interminably. She needed to speak with him.

"How nice," she said. "But I'm afraid I'm busy."

Mrs. Feldman's eyes widened, and her mouth formed an *o*. "Indeed."

"Yes." Leonora nodded hastily. "I—er—can't explain. How nice to see you though."

With that, Leonora barreled through the throng of perfume- and cologne-dabbed men and women sporting velvet-and-silk attire.

Finally, she spotted Sebastian. She gave him her best regal smile, ignoring the pitter-patter of her heart.

THE ROOM BRIMMED with Sebastian's friends. He should have been laughing with them and telling them stories.

Instead, he was dancing with Miss Daphne Richmond. Though Miss Richmond did not step on Sebastian's foot a single time and had a pleasant visage and amiable demeanor, Leonora remained in Sebastian's mind.

Leonora was mesmerizing. The manner in which she flung her long white neck back when she laughed was enchanting, and he had the horrible suspicion he was not merely fascinated by the way in which her ruby necklace nestled in the hollow of her collar.

The whole thing was dreadful. An absence of education that would have made every one of his tutors at Oxford scoff and would have all the previous Dukes of Dartmouth writhing in their graves.

Unfortunately, she was also here, at this blasted ball. Her sleek dress highlighted her sumptuous skin. The red color was darker than the rest of the dresses at the ball, whose owners had chosen pastel pinks and blues, and apple greens, when they'd not clothed themselves in ivory. There was something serious and solemn in her gaze that made Sebastian's chest tighten. Her elegant dress swathed her tall figure, nestling about her bosom and hips.

Another, more sentimental man would immediately have termed Leonora a goddess or queen.

Obviously, Sebastian did not succumb to such audacities of emotion. His cock twitched, and he scowled.

He needed this to end.

Leonora strode toward him. No doubt she wasn't actually going to speak to him. Conversations were things Leonora and he no longer did. Sebastian braced himself for exchanging barbs.

"You're smiling," Miss Richmond murmured.

"I am?"

"Indeed."

"I—er—like this dance," Sebastian muttered, grateful when it ended. He made another comment on the overall agreeableness of the cotillion, then strode toward Leonora.

He needed to speak to her. She knew something about Mimi's presence, he was certain.

He enjoyed the manner in which her eyes widened, as if calculating the other people with whom he might desire to speak.

Then he swept into a deep bow. Her cheeks pinkened, and Sebastian grinned. He liked that he was making her feel uncomfortable.

"May I have this dance, Miss Holt?" he asked.

Her eyes widened.

"You can't be so surprised someone would desire to dance with you."

Her cheeks flamed, though this time he was certain it was with anger.

Good.

Any emotion besides anger somehow seemed dangerous, at least when it had to do with her.

She gritted her teeth, then took his hand. Dancers swirled around them.

Mighty Poseidon.

The violinists had started playing a waltz. Of all the dances for them to choose, they'd had to do the most intimate one.

Never mind that.

Every married couple in the room seemed determined to choose this particular dance. They gazed cow-eyed at each other, the women's lashes fluttering and the men beaming, as if already imagining being in bed with their wives.

"Can you explain why you had someone pose as Lady Seneca Footwall?"

Leonora stiffened in his arms, and his lips twitched.

He leaned toward her, ignoring the delicious rose scent that wafted about her. "What are you playing at?"

Chapter Six

Leonora knew Sebastian had only whispered the words, but they seemed to thunder.

"I know," he said.

She did her best to feign innocence. "What do you know, Your Grace?"

He raised an eyebrow. "When have you ever called me Your Grace?"

"I make it a point to call you very little," Leonora said.

For a moment, Sebastian was silent. He weaved her about the room, twirling her in his arms. Her head felt light as she spun, and she became dizzy.

"How do you know Mimi?" he asked.

Leonora's heartbeat quickened. Sebastian knew Mimi? The room warmed, and sweat beaded over the nape of her neck.

Heavens. That explained his aloofness around Mimi. Sebastian had recognized her. No wonder he'd stayed away from her.

Just because Timothy was not fond of the theater didn't mean all aristocrats shared his indifference. Her heart thrummed. She'd even wondered if Sebastian was not like other men, or at least, not like other wicked men. But now it was clear she had been right about him all along.

Sebastian was so taken with actresses he was on a first-name basis with them, could recognize them without their makeup and wigs. *Heavens!* Did he know Mimi *intimately*? The thought entered Leonora's mind, and her shoulders tensed as she pondered the possibility of Sebastian moving his succulent lips over Mimi's skin.

When Sebastian closed his eyes, did visions of Mimi enter his mind? Did he yearn for her? Did he crave her? The world tilted precariously. Visions of Sebastian removing his shirt and revealing his sculpted body filled Leonora's mind. Would he have carried Mimi in his large, sturdy arms? What did men do with the women they admired, that they lusted for? Her heartbeat quickened anew, and the space between her legs suddenly seemed damp.

She forced her chin to remain high. "I have no idea what you're speaking about."

Sebastian's eyes glinted coldly. She shuddered, and his smile widened.

Leonora had to think quickly. Apparently, Sebastian was familiar with actresses and opera singers. Even disguises didn't tamper his knowledge. She should have suspected he would be familiar with people associated with disrepute, even though he'd acted haughtily at her mother's scandal.

She tightened her fists automatically. How could she get him to ruin his reputation but leave hers intact? When would she have the chance to dance with him otherwise?

Then the idea came to her. She would have to make certain to show people how improper he was, even if she did it herself. Perhaps she could get him to touch her inappropriately—if he did that in front of a crowd, he'd be seen as the aggressor. No one could term her wanton then.

Leonora suddenly missed a step. "My ankle! I've turned it. I'm so sorry, Your Grace."

Sebastian halted dancing. A few people peered at them, though they continued to swirl about with such force that Leonora worried they might barrel into them.

"Let me help you to a chair, my lady," Sebastian said smoothly.

She hobbled across the floor.

This was the moment.

Leonora gritted her teeth, then swayed dramatically. If she could just have him touch her bosom when he caught her, she could besmirch his reputation. He would be taking advantage of a practical invalid. His arms reached for her, and she smiled.

Success was upon her.

In the next moment, she tipped too far in the other direction. Sebastian grabbed both her arms to keep her upright. Unfortunately, neither arm was near her bosom. She'd only managed to humiliate herself, and a sharp pain moved through her ankle.

Heavens, now she'd *actually* managed to injure herself. Worse, he hadn't grabbed her in an inappropriate manner at all. His reputation remained pristine.

The duke guided her into a chair. "That was nearly quite a tumble."

"My ankle was injured," she said.

"And now you're favoring the other one." He raised an eyebrow, and her heart sank. *Heavens*. Had he known exactly what she'd attempted to do?

She raised her chin. "I must have turned both of them."

"For a woman who has turned both ankles, you are doing a magnificent job of walking."

Her skin heated, and she gritted her teeth.

The duke helped her into a chair by the fireplace, between two matronly women. "Dancing is not for everyone, Miss Holt."

"Thank you," she mumbled.

Sebastian swept into an elegant bow, and Leonora's face burned.

The matronly women turned their wrinkled faces toward her, and one of them removed a monocle from her reticule to gaze in the direction of Leonora's ankle.

"Not a good dancer?" the other woman murmured, raising a thin gray eyebrow.

"What a silly question!" the woman with the monocle exclaimed. "Naturally, she's a terrible dancer. Even my Henrietta never managed to turn her ankle. And she was incredibly ungifted. I must mention this to her the next time I see her. She'll be relieved to know she's no longer the most dreadful dancer of the *ton*."

"She's awfully pretty to be a bad dancer," the other woman observed, raking her gaze over Leonora's body with the efficiency of a modiste in want of measuring tape.

"She probably didn't pay attention in dance class," the woman with the monocle huffed. "That was Henrietta's problem."

"Ah." The other woman wrinkled her nose, and the kindly expression in her face disappeared. "One must pay attention to one's lessons."

Leonora fought tears of humiliation as Sebastian strolled further and further away.

LAST NIGHT HAD been dashed odd. Sebastian had thought about Leonora for a higher proportion of the day than he desired to admit. Obviously, that had simply been because he'd had the distinct impression she'd arranged to have Mimi at the ball, then denied any acquaintance with her. Mysteries, after all, were worth pondering.

Sebastian had absolutely not been contemplating Leonora for any other reason. That would be absurd, and Sebastian made a point of not embracing absurdity unnecessarily.

No. There was one person he needed to speak to, and he knew just where to find her.

"I'll require my carriage," he told his butler.

"Very well, Your Grace. The usual destination?"

"Indeed."

His butler nodded, an image of discretion.

In truth, though there was nothing particularly unusual about his destination for members of the *ton*, there was something decidedly unusual about the frequency with which he visited.

Covent Garden was a place high society ventured to at night to indulge in a musical performance but forgot during the day, leaving its bustling market to their servants. The grimy taverns and seedy establishments frequented by men in search of a woman to bed were best viewed at night from a briskly moving carriage.

The carriage ride to Covent Garden was probably not any longer than customary, yet today, the ride seemed to stretch ceaselessly. Sebastian was conscious of each shouting hack driver determined to quicken his speed, each plodding cow, each man pushing a wheelbarrow, and each oversize and overdecorated barouche determined to glide at a glacial pace in order for the people on the pavement to best admire it.

Sebastian murmured goodbye to his driver, then marched inside the Theatre Royal. A few people nodded at him absent-mindedly. They recognized him but didn't know his title. Sebastian had always been careful to not accept invitations to performances here from members of the *ton*. He didn't want this particular world to collide with his ducal one. No one needed to think they might ever take advantage of him.

Like they had Papa.

Sebastian grimaced as he strode toward Mimi's room. He knocked on the door, then entered.

Mimi sighed when she saw him. "I was wondering when you would show up."

"Am I that predictable?"

She shrugged nonchalantly.

"You were in disguise," he told Mimi.

"I know." Mimi frowned and concentrated on her reflection in her dressing table mirror.

"Why did you call yourself by that ridiculous name?"

"I was acting." Mimi powdered her face.

"Who hired you?"

Mimi was silent.

"Did Miss Leonora Holt have anything to do with your appearance?"

"A debutante?" Mimi smiled. "That would be very uncharacteristic behavior for a young lady of the *ton*."

Sebastian sighed.

Mimi was right.

Damnation. Of course Leonora couldn't have had anything to do with it.

He tilted his head. "Was it Lord Richmond?"

Mimi blinked and squirmed in her seat. "That is confidential."

"Lord Richmond was the host," Sebastian said, still staring at Mimi.

"Indeed." Mimi patted her face with greater force, and powder spewed into the air.

Mimi glanced at him. "What exactly is your relationship with Miss Holt?"

Sebastian frowned. "I don't have one."

"I see," Mimi said, though the words had none of her customary force.

He jerked his head toward her. "What makes you ask?"

"I thought it odd you suspected she might be involved in my presence last night."

"Oh." Sebastian blinked. "I suppose that makes sense."

"Of course it does." Mimi gave him a bright smile, then her face sobered. "You haven't *harmed* her or anything?"

Sebastian's eyes widened. "Naturally not. There are family differences. That's all."

Mimi bit her lip and surveyed him. Sebastian frowned.

"She's quite pretty," Mimi said.

"I suppose she's tolerable," Sebastian said mildly, but something in his chest tightened, and he averted his gaze hastily, lest Mimi be able to read something on his face.

"Why do you have it in for those girls?"

Sebastian exhaled. The world was suddenly less spectacular. Father should be here, and he wasn't.

"Their father cheated during a card game, and my father lost prime land to him," Sebastian muttered. "That land was needed to keep everything going."

"I never thought you were in financial difficulties." Mimi shifted in her seat, as if the very mention of the topic was sufficient to void the leather chair of its sumptuous qualities.

"I'm not." Sebastian scowled. "I managed to rebuild everything. Damned hard though."

"Then there is no problem."

Sebastian clenched his fists. "A cheat is a cheat. Since their father is dead, the daughters will have to pay."

"Are you certain?"

"Of course I'm certain. Besides, Miss Leonora Holt knew about the cheating. She refuses to mention it." He swallowed hard, remembering Leonora's defense of her father on that terrible day.

"I see."

An awkward silence pervaded.

"I know you disapprove," Sebastian said.

"Then I'll spare you a recital of my exact opinion. Though, you should reconsider."

"I won't."

She sighed. "The placards for *The Bewitched Throne* will be painted next month."

"Oh?"

"If you want your name—"

"I don't," Sebastian said shortly.

He would never accomplish as much as he did if people knew he devoted so much time to composing music. Music was deemed frivolous. Something to be admired but better suited to the continental people who toured England on occasion. There were few English composers here.

Sebastian's operas with their lurid love scenarios and abundance of villains might make people view him in an altogether inappropriate manner. He was in Parliament, after all. No, Sebastian needed to be respected. That was vital. If people didn't respect him, they might gain the confidence to try to steal his estate, just as Leonora's father had once done.

"Very well, *Anonymous*." Mimi grinned. "You should be very grateful your music is so wonderful."

Sebastian smirked. "It is rather wonderful, isn't it?"

Mimi rolled her eyes, but she did not contradict him. No one could.

Chapter Seven

Leonora hobbled to the drawing room, making use of the banister.

Timothy and Constance eyed her swollen ankle.

"I thought Mrs. Feldman trained you better at dancing," Timothy said. "What did she think we were paying her for in that finishing school?"

Leonora gave a wobbly smile. "It was an accident."

"Waltzing is not normally the place for accidents. Thank goodness Dartmouth could assist you. Perhaps I've been underestimating him."

Leonora's eyes widened as she stared at her brother.

"I suppose we'll see more of him, given his friendship with Sabrina's betrothed," Timothy added.

Leonora squirmed. "We shouldn't see him. He shouldn't have attended Eloisa's wedding. That painting—"

Timothy shook his head. "I hope you're not going to tell us again *he* put it there. It's insane to antagonize the duke whose property borders ours. The only person who benefited from the display was Julius. He received even more publicity for his art."

"Perhaps it wasn't wise to invite so many people," Constance said.

"It was important to show we are reestablished in society," Timothy declared.

"You have a guest," the butler said in his normal, regal tone.

"I do?" Leonora squeaked, and Constance clapped her hands. She elbowed Timothy. "It must be Mrs. Feldman's nephew!"

Timothy beamed. "You finally have a suitor. Both your sisters have found men to spend the rest of their lives with. Now, do you remember your lessons from finishing school?"

"O-Of course."

"It is a female guest," the butler interjected.

"Ah, not a future husband," Timothy said.

"It would seem not," the butler said tersely. He paused. "But perhaps a future lifelong companion."

"Oh." Timothy blinked, and Leonora's skin heated.

"I am not searching for a lifelong companion," she said stiffly.

"Well, you don't seem to be doing much searching for a husband." Bitterness permeated her brother's voice, and Constance elbowed him hard.

Leonora had spent so much time thinking about Sebastian she hadn't considered who would make a good prospect. Matrimony was the foremost goal of every debutante, but most debutantes didn't have the Duke of Dartmouth to worry about.

She wondered who had come to visit her. Why hadn't the butler given a name? He knew most of her friends. They had visited from time to time before the season began officially, before that first horrible ball when Mama's painting had been revealed and Leonora and her sisters had become tarnished with scandal.

Leonora stumbled into the entry, pulling her bad ankle behind her.

There before her was Mimi.

Mimi handed a small satchel to Leonora. Coins clinked. "I wanted to return this."

"That is unnecessary." Leonora bit her lip. "My plan was imperfect. The duke suspected."

Mimi shook her head. "You should have it."

Leonora took the bag reluctantly.

"I couldn't do it. I-I know him," Mimi said. "I'm sorry."

A chill descended through the room. Leonora was suddenly exceedingly aware that there was no fireplace in the foyer.

Then, it was true. Sebastian was one of those men who visited opera singers. Or had Mimi simply meant she'd been intimidated by his position?

"You saw his picture in the broadsheets?" she asked.

"Yes." For some odd reason, the broadsheets referred to the duke in fawning terms when they devoted articles to him. They spoke about his work in Parliament with enthusiasm. No doubt his position inspired sycophancy.

"Though if he hadn't known who *I* was—"

"He did?" Leonora asked faintly.

Mimi nodded. *Heavens*. Mimi was pretty, and Sebastian was an unattached man. Not that being attached was something that prevented men from frequenting beautiful women. Everyone knew men were prone to visit courtesans. At her finishing school, Leonora had been taught men had many physical needs and that such visits were to be of no concern.

Indeed, some older married women had lovers on the side, indulging in their own desires after they had given birth to the requisite heirs and spares and could finally consider what they truly wanted in life. Often, what they truly wanted in life were fresh-faced footmen and broad-shouldered grooms. People jested about it at parties.

"Not like that," Mimi said, evidently seeing something in Leonora's face. "He's a good man."

Leonora rolled her eyes. "You have no idea."

"But I do," Mimi said. "I think you should reconsider your plan."

"I won't be able to do anything now," Leonora said.

"G-Good. He really is admirable."

"How nice." Leonora didn't bother to paste a smile on her face. The last thing Leonora wanted to do was discuss the duke's merits.

"I should go," Mimi said.

"Indeed," Leonora concurred.

Mimi looked like she might want to say more, then left. The door closed, and Leonora returned to Constance and Timothy.

"Who was it?" Constance asked.

"Just a friend," Leonora lied.

Constance's eyes narrowed, but Timothy simply shrugged.

"I thought it might have been Mrs. Feldman," he said.

"Mrs. Feldman?" Leonora's eyebrows jolted up. Leonora had attended Mrs. Feldman's finishing school. She'd spent most of the time avoiding Mrs. Feldman. She certainly hadn't expected Mrs. Feldman to visit.

"Yes. She was concerned with you."

"Oh." Leonora bit her lip. Leonora had prided herself on being a good student at finishing school. She hadn't expected to have no suitors so late in the season. She'd been an excellent student, and sufficiently pretty and accomplished to expect to have her pick of suitors. But that had been *before*.

"Perhaps we shouldn't have waited to give you a season with your sisters."

"Are you referring to the fact I'm older than other debutantes?"

Timothy nodded matter-of-factly, and Leonora shuddered. She didn't feel older. In fact, she didn't even think she looked older than them, but perhaps others could tell. A sour taste invaded her throat.

"We want you to find a husband," Timothy said. "You were supposed to be the easiest to match."

"But I am proving difficult," she said flatly.

"*Difficult* isn't a term we like," Constance said quickly.

"But perhaps it's the right term." Timothy gave Leonora an approving nod. "She understands. Anyway, we'll go out of London for a while."

"Indeed?" Constance asked.

"Yes," Timothy nodded. "Some people are having a house

party. It might be nice to get away from the balls." He glanced at Leonora's ankle. "Particularly considering your imperfect dance skills."

<hr />

SEBASTIAN STRODE INTO Robertson's Gentlemen's Club and sank into his favorite chair. The glossy red leather met all its promises of comfort, and contentment wafted over him, lulled by the hum of baritone and tenor voices.

Glossy blond strands peaked from a nearby newspaper, and Percival's head appeared. Percival folded his paper, then plopped into the seat next to Sebastian.

"Good afternoon," Sebastian said lightly.

"Your butler told me I would find you here," Percival said.

"Indeed?"

"But you only arrived now."

"Oh." Sebastian shifted his legs. "My driver must have taken the long way again."

"How curious," Percival remarked dryly, then pressed his lips together. "I didn't want to say anything in front of Cornelius, but we both know you're responsible for that painting."

Sebastian widened his eyes. "I wouldn't—"

Percival raised his eyebrow. "Don't lie to me."

Sebastian slumped his shoulders. "I'm sorry. You're correct. You're my best friend."

"And you used my fiancée's sister's wedding as a place to stage some absurd revenge on the Holt family."

Sebastian stiffened. "It's not absurd. My father would have lived longer if he hadn't been cheated by that cruel family. He died worried about the future of the estate."

"An estate you've recovered."

"I was lucky. If the weather had been terrible—"

"You would have figured something out," Percival finished

for him. "You always do."

"Naturally."

"You're lucky you didn't pull that despicable act at my wedding," Percival said. "And you're lucky Leonora was able to distract the guests and bride with her music. I don't know what would have happened without her quick thinking. No one would want to hear me recite Shakespeare's sonnets, that's for certain."

An odd feeling formed in Sebastian's chest. A feeling that felt terribly like guilt. A feeling he didn't like in the least.

"You need to get along with Leonora. I'm going to marry Sabrina. You're going to see each other. You're going to see the whole family."

"But—"

Percival fixed Sebastian with an uncharacteristically firm stare, and Sebastian's shoulders slumped.

"Fine," he muttered. "But only because you're correct."

Percival smirked, and Sebastian glowered at his dearest friend.

He needed to fix this.

Now.

Percival was acting as if Sebastian was the enemy, even though Sebastian was his best friend.

"I had already come to that realization," Sebastian lied.

Percival's lips twitched. "Had you?"

Sebastian jutted his chin up.

"In fact, I wanted to invite you to a house party I'm having," Sebastian declared. "I would like you to attend."

"I always attend your springtime house party," Percival said. "Though, I might be busy this year."

"I know," Sebastian agreed. "You have obligations with your betrothed's family. But actually, I would like to invite Sabrina and her entire family."

Percival widened his eyes. "You don't happen to mean her *whole* family?"

"That's precisely what I mean." Sebastian nodded an unnecessary number of times. "I need to make peace with them. In fact, if they have any suggestions for anyone else I should invite, please let me know."

"Oh." Percival frowned. "That's very nice of you."

"I am very nice," Sebastian insisted.

Besides, Percival was right. Percival was his dearest friend, and he didn't want to lose him just because of his association with the dreaded Holts. Sebastian had done everything in his power to warn Percival against the Holt family, but the man was determined to marry into it.

Besides, perhaps a house party wouldn't be dreadful. His castle was large. He could have his servants bring him breakfast in his room and imbibe enough wine and brandy he wouldn't even want to strangle Timothy.

Actually, Sebastian wasn't certain he would want to strangle Timothy even if he was subsisting on fewer alcoholic-filled drink compilations. Timothy wasn't the same boy who'd used to remind everyone of his advanced age. His wife, Constance, certainly seemed sensible. He doubted Timothy would want to put frogs anywhere inside the house.

No, he would be generous and forgiving. Sebastian smiled. He would confuse them, and that was just fine. "I look forward to spending time with them."

"Truly?" Percival tilted his head as if Sebastian was a misbehaving child who required frequent scoldings and as if Percival was not sure whether this occasion necessitated the beech or not.

"Naturally," Sebastian said. "Besides, Leonora and I were once close."

That had been when he was ten, and ten-year-olds were never much lauded for their intelligence.

Still, it had been the case. Every day after he'd finished his lessons with his tutors, he'd run into the wooded area between their two homes and waited for her to appear at the lake. Then they'd talked and played for hours until the sun made its descent.

It had been the best part of his childhood.

"It would be nice to reacquaint myself with her," Sebastian added.

Oddly, that statement felt true. It would be nice to get to know Leonora better. In a strange manner, she was even fascinating.

Percival nodded perfunctorily. "Very well."

"My butler will send some invitations," Sebastian said. "Then I look forward to seeing you. And do let me know if there's anyone else they want to spend time with."

Percival frowned. "Timothy did mention a Lord Knightley."

"Ah." Sebastian nodded. That must be one of Timothy's friends. "Very well. He's invited also."

Sebastian leaned back, enjoying his friend's startled expression.

Chapter Eight

Two weeks later

"I hear a carriage," the butler said.

"Splendid," Sebastian said weakly.

Inviting the entire Holt family had seemed a much better idea earlier. Now he was far less certain. *Damnation.* Well, there was nothing to be done about it.

He turned to his butler. "Please see to it that my breakfast is brought up to my room in the morning."

"You did mention that before."

"Good, good," Sebastian said.

"I should tell the servants the carriage is arriving," the butler said.

"Of course. Quite right. We wouldn't want Mr. Holt to not be greeted. The point is to dazzle him."

"We can do that, Your Grace."

"And that's why you're the butler," Sebastian said, forcing his voice to sound cheerful, despite the fact his heart was beating with an uncomfortable rapidity.

"Indeed, Your Grace."

Sebastian sighed. "I suppose I should go outside as well."

"Fresh air is always beneficial, Your Grace. At least, when it's not raining."

"Or snowing."

"Or snowing, Your Grace."

Sebastian gave a strained nod.

Normally he wasn't this nervous. He steeled his fists. He was not going to flinch before Timothy or Leonora.

The carriage crunched over the gravel, drawn by four white horses.

Sebastian wondered whether Timothy always took carriages drawn by four white horses, or if he'd hired the horses especially for this occasion.

The driver glided to the carriage door and opened it. Timothy and his wife stepped outside.

"Mr. Holt," Sebastian said, emphasizing the attribute. Timothy's father might have taken Sebastian's best land, but at least he couldn't carry off with the title.

Then Leonora, Sabrina, and Percival exited.

Another carriage pulled up, containing Cornelius, his new wife, and Mrs. Holt and Julius Stanwycke.

Sebastian avoided eye contact with Leonora, despising the manner his heart quickened.

"Sebastian! Darling boy!" Mrs. Holt waved her arm and grinned.

Sebastian smiled back. Even though much of society now despised Mrs. Holt, he'd always found her charming.

Her joviality was contagious.

Mrs. Holt hadn't always been accompanied by a tall, handsome artist. Sebastian was used to seeing her with her perpetually sour-faced late husband. Lately, though, everything had changed.

"I didn't know you would be here." Sebastian bowed obediently.

"I'm an unexpected pleasure," Mrs. Holt declared, and Sebastian chuckled.

"Indeed, you are."

Mrs. Holt leaned nearer him. "It was very naughty of you to gift Eloisa that painting of me."

"I'm sure I don't know what you're speaking about," Sebastian said.

Mrs. Holt shook her head, but her eyes sparkled. Lately, Mrs. Holt's eyes were always sparkling.

He turned to Julius. "How nice to see you again."

"Indeed, Your Grace." Julius sniffed. "I don't normally spend time with aristocrats."

"Yes, you're being quite daring," Sebastian teased.

"Good afternoon, Dartmouth," Timothy said. "Has Lord Knightley appeared yet?"

"Not yet," Sebastian said.

"He will," Timothy said.

Sebastian smiled. He hadn't expected Timothy to be so eager to see his friend. Perhaps Timothy was also nervous about this house party. Sebastian put his arm on Timothy's back. "Let me show you inside."

OF ALL THE invitations to accept, Timothy had to accept Sebastian's. Leonora shuddered. If only her plan had worked. She avoided speaking with Sebastian, a fact made easier by the fact that he also seemed to be avoiding her. *Well.* She couldn't blame him for that.

She glanced at her sisters, but they were busy staring sentimentally at their beloveds.

"Let's explore the garden!" Sabrina explained.

The others concurred.

"Coming, Leonora?" Eloisa asked.

"Eventually."

The others hurried outside.

Wandering rose gardens was less intriguing when one could happen upon a dewy-eyed couple at any moment. Leonora was too wise to attempt to venture into the maze when Sabrina and

Eloisa were strolling about with their beloveds. The viscount and earl were prone to abruptly reciting Sabrina's and Eloisa's charms with sentimental zeal best confined to leather-bound poetry books.

Leonora decided to explore the castle. She started in the great hall, admiring its medieval furniture and tapestries. She turned into a corridor, striding past portraits of long-dead ancestors. Most gazed at her from frilly collars, while others were arranged in full family portraits beside picturesque trees.

Leonora continued past these pictures of idyllic happiness, until she came to an open door leading to a library. Though the books that lined the walls might have sufficed in drawing her attention, no leather-bound book, no matter the manner in which its typography glittered, could compare to the grand piano that sat in the room. Leonora's fingers itched to play, and she stepped inside, ignoring the musky scent of imposing tomes.

The glossy black piano gleamed enticingly, and she hurried toward it. She played some Mozart, then halted. Was there sheet music in the room? There was some music in a basket near the piano, and she flipped absentmindedly through the pages until she came to some handwritten compositions.

Who had written this? Leonora took the handwritten sheet, placed it on the piano, and played. She played and played and played. The music drifted over her in a pleasing fashion.

Footsteps sounded outside, but she continued to play. The afternoon was much more pleasant than she'd anticipated.

"Stop that." A baritone voice interrupted her music, and she turned her head.

Sebastian.

The duke glowered at her. His eyes blazed, and Leonora moved her fingers from the keys, as if they'd burned her.

She'd been so focused on the music she was surprised to find herself not alone.

"I didn't hear you enter," she said.

Sebastian made no effort to apologize for startling her. Instead, he marched toward her. His Hessians thumped over the wooden floorboards and echoed through the room. For the first time, she wished the acoustics in this room were not nearly as wonderful after all.

He continued to near her, and his cotton scent wafted about her nostrils. Then Sebastian stretched down in front of her. For a wild moment, she thought he might kiss her. For an even wilder moment, she thought she might want that. Instead, he simply snatched her piano sheets, then held them against his chest.

She narrowed her eyes. "What are you doing? I was playing."

"That was obvious."

Leonora knitted her brows. "And I'm not allowed to play?"

"Not this."

She rose, hating that he was still a full four inches taller than her. Normally she was very tall. She was taller than either of her sisters and even equaled Timothy in height. But Sebastian still soared above her, and she craned her neck to see his angrily flashing eyes.

"I can play what I desire."

"That was private." His eyes pierced hers, and his lofty size seemed designed to intimidate warriors.

Not that she was a warrior.

Leonora despised him. She'd been enjoying herself, and he'd come and ruined everything.

She crossed her arms and did her best impression of an angry ogre. "It was there with everything else."

Something like guilt flickered over his face, but he jutted out his jaw. "It was handwritten. You shouldn't play handwritten music. That means it might not be finished."

"It sounded perfectly fine."

"I doubt the composer would have appreciated you to play half-finished work."

"Why do you care what the composer thinks?"

He averted his eyes, and then a thought occurred to her, an odd thought, a thought that made absolutely no sense in the world. And yet the question hung on her lips. "You wrote that."

Sebastian stepped back, and his gaze remained focused on the floorboards.

She rolled her eyes. "There's not even a carpet there for you to pretend to be admiring. You can look at me."

He jerked his head to her, clearly irritated. His face was redder than before, and the pupils of his eyes looked larger. "Don't order me around."

"Why don't you answer my question?" She stopped, and his scent drifted around her in that intoxicating manner again. *Heavens.* Why did the man have to be so appealing? Why was his jaw so sturdy? Why were his shoulders so broad? And why on earth were his lips so utterly succulent? He glared at her from beneath his long eyelashes, and she rose on her tiptoes.

Then she kissed him.

At least, she must have kissed him.

Their lips were touching. In the next moment, he wrapped his large, sturdy arms about her, pushing her against his firm chest. Her heartbeat surged.

Carriage wheels crunched on the gravel outside the castle. And shortly after, murmurings came from downstairs. The sounds made her step back.

His eyes were still wide. "You kissed me."

Drat.

She had done that.

He continued to stare. "Why did you do that?"

"It didn't mean anything." The words tumbled out, and his face stiffened.

"I suspected that," he said, his voice filled with wry humor she wasn't sure he actually meant.

"You stood so near me," she said. "You invaded my space. It was instinct."

"I see. Do you often go around kissing people who stand near you?"

Leonora's skin heated. She turned around abruptly.

"One wonders what it might be like to stand beside you during the crush to enter certain balls," he continued.

"I'm sorry," she said and closed her eyes. Embarrassment filled her. "Normally I don't go around kissing people."

"Because there's typically more distance between people and you?"

"No," she admitted, and his lips curled into a predictable, ever-so-irritating smirk.

She loathed him.

"We're still standing very close," he reminded her.

"I know," she said, and her voice wobbled. Only centimeters separated them. She stared at him.

"You're older than you used to be," she observed, then her cheeks heated.

The statement was absurd.

But then, a decade ago they'd played together every day.

He nodded solemnly, as if she'd said something insightful.

"So are you, and you're…" He hesitated, then closed his mouth.

Leonora wondered what he'd wanted to say. She had the vague impression he might have been thinking about her figure, and warmth rushed through her.

"Do you remember the last time?" he asked.

"You were with your father."

He shook his head. "No, I didn't mean the last time we saw each other since we were younger. I meant the last time we really were together."

"Oh. That was probably at the lake."

He nodded.

"There were many fallen leaves."

"Indeed."

For an odd moment, she could almost feel the leaves crunching beneath her, but then she realized she was probably just swaying. Something about Sebastian made her tilt off-balance.

"You're not as proper as you seem," Sebastian said, and his

eyes darkened.

Leonora stepped back. "I'm sure I don't know what you mean."

She forced her lips into a smile, which only made Sebastian's eyebrows narrow.

Drat.

She should have remembered she never smiled in Sebastian's presence. No doubt he would find that alone to be suspicious.

"Is something troubling you, Your Grace?" she asked. "Perhaps I should call for a maid."

"I should call for everyone so they can hear what you did."

Leonora's throat dried, but she forced her face to remain calm, or as calm as possible. No one could know she'd hired an actress. She shouldn't even be seen talking with actresses. It wasn't the sort of thing respectable women were prone to doing.

"Excuse me," she said, but she was certain her voice was an octave higher than normal. Sebastian smirked.

Why did he have to be so handsome when his lips moved in that manner? She'd never considered lips to be succulent, but lately, she had been wondering what they might taste like, what they might feel like against her own.

"Mimi is an actress who looks remarkably like Lady Seneca Footwall."

Leonora forced herself to have an innocent expression on her face. "Indeed? I suppose Lady Seneca will be flattered to hear that. Assuming, of course, that this Mimi is popular with audiences."

"Oh yes," Sebastian said icily. "Very popular."

She swallowed hard and shot him a wobbly smile.

"How are you feeling?" Sebastian asked.

"Fine," she squeaked.

"Are you certain you're not unwell, Miss Holt?" Sebastian's voice remained saccharine. "Perhaps spurred by a guilty conscience?"

Leonora stiffened. "I have no idea what you're talking about."

"You hired Mimi to play the role of Lady Seneca Footwall."

Leonora's jaw dropped. He knew! How did he know? Surely Mimi hadn't told him?

"You're stunned I figured it out."

"N-No," she managed to stammer. "I am astounded you should think such a thing! What an abomination! What would I ever know about actresses?"

Sebastian frowned, and Leonora's shoulders eased. He didn't know. Mimi hadn't told him. It was all a hypothesis.

She raised her chin. "That is an utterly absurd statement. Besides, if this Lady Seneca Footwall was an impostor, why did you not tell Lord and Lady Richmond? Surely that would be the proper thing to do?"

"Well, I…" Sebastian was silent, and his eyes darted from side to side.

"I have a mind to tell them myself."

"Oh no," Sebastian said, "that's unnecessary."

"I think they would be concerned some person from the stage was gallivanting around in their ball under a name of some aristocrat. In fact, I would imagine the Footwalls themselves would be quite taken aback. I will write them a letter immediately." Leonora picked up a quill.

"I might have made a mistake. Perhaps she simply resembled an actress."

"I see you're around so many actresses you've forgotten some people are not on the stage. That some people have morals."

Sebastian swallowed hard. "I wouldn't say people on the stage lack morals."

"That is comforting." Leonora set her quill down. "I suppose everyone seems to have morals when compared to you."

Sebastian was silent, and an odd guilt surged through Leonora.

"You never did show me how to fish," she said, striving to focus on something besides his general handsomeness and the fact she'd just done something terribly scandalous.

"I can show you." A cloud formed over his face. Perhaps he remembered they despised each other.

She shrugged. "It wouldn't be horrible."

His face brightened. "No," he agreed. "Perhaps not."

"Miss Holt!" A parlor maid ducked her head into the library. Her eyes widened when she saw Sebastian, and Leonora smoothed her attire hastily before dropping her hands. No doubt attire smoothing in the presence of a handsome man might be deemed suspicious behavior.

"There is a guest in the drawing room. Your brother asked me to find you."

"I see."

"Should I come as well?" Sebastian asked.

"I-I suppose so," the maid stammered, her skin pinkening.

Leonora didn't blame her. Sebastian was very handsome, though she would have expected the maid to be aware of that by this point. Surely nothing else might be unsettling her?

"Very well." Leonora strolled out of the library, conscious of Sebastian beside her.

She opened the drawing room door and strode through it. Green pillows dotted the green sofa, which mirrored the green wallpaper. She suspected some enthusiastic decorator had recommended green to give the appearance of nature during the cold winter months.

Timothy smiled when they entered. Beside Timothy was another man, one she did not recognize.

The man had blond hair and was gazing at her intently.

"You must be Lord Knightley," Sebastian said. "Mr. Holt's friend."

Lord Knightley raised his eyebrows. "Oh, no, Mr. Holt and I have just met."

Sebastian frowned.

"My aunt insisted I come," Lord Knightley explained.

"I see," Sebastian said uncertainly.

"It's quite hard to be able to see Leonora Holt," Lord Knightley said.

"Me?" Leonora's eyes widened. It was impossible to ignore the manner in which Timothy gestured to Leonora to draw nearer, as if he was offering up a particularly nice serving of caviar to the viscount. It was equally impossible to ignore Lord Knightley's calculating look at Leonora, and she shivered.

"Your Grace. I did not expect to see you here," Timothy said icily, after everyone had exchanged the appropriate introductions.

"Well, that's what happens when I'm the host," Sebastian said lightly and plopped into a chair. "You're bound to see me on occasion."

Timothy's eyebrows narrowed, but thankfully he dropped the subject. Leonora hardly wanted Timothy to know Sebastian and she had been alone.

Timothy's eyes glimmered, and he waved his hand with a flourish toward the viscount. "My sister is still unmarried."

Leonora jerked her legs toward her chair involuntarily.

Lord Knightley was a tall blond man with bright-blue eyes. He looked like he'd stepped from one of the medieval tapestries that hung in the great hall. He was also a full twenty years older than Leonora.

"I'm going to explore the grounds," Sebastian said curtly, then marched off suddenly. Leonora stared after him for a moment.

Timothy gave a terse smile. "I'm afraid he's a bit rude."

"Oh, I understand," Lord Knightley said. "Some people are cranky. Perhaps he's one of those people who sleeps poorly."

"And you're not one of those people?" Constance asked.

"Oh no, I make a point of doing everything well."

Timothy beamed. *Oh, heavens.* Why was Timothy grinning in that manner? Did he consider himself a matchmaker? Leonora shot a horrified look at her brother, but he was indeed still smiling.

"I'm so glad you were able to visit," Timothy said.

"I like to make my aunt happy."

"Who is your aunt?" Leonora asked.

"Mrs. Feldman," Lord Knightley said.

"Mrs. Feldman?" Leonora's eyes widened. Mrs. Feldman had run Mrs. Feldman's School for Remarkable Young Ladies, where Leonora had just spent most of her recent years. "You're *that* Lord Knightley."

"Mm-hmm." Lord Knightley's chest puffed out.

"She's spoken about you before. I should have recognized your name."

"A great memory is not one of the most important things to have," he said soothingly, "particularly when one is imbued with great beauty."

Timothy's lips stretched up even wider. Leonora hadn't seen her brother so happy for years, perhaps not since his wedding day. Leonora forced her attention onto the viscount and tried not to think of her very first kiss.

Chapter Nine

The rest of the day was less exhilarating. Sebastian should be happy someone was here to distract Leonora. Most likely she wouldn't be going around kissing him in music rooms, then.

He dwelled on the memory of the kiss, even as people chattered about him in the drawing room. Perhaps she'd kissed him accidentally, but that didn't hinder her taste from lingering on his lips. If he concentrated, he could still remember the exact texture of her luscious pout.

"We should have music." Sabrina clapped her hands.

A shudder went down Sebastian's spine. This was not the first house party he'd held where someone had suggested there be music. Unfortunately, despite the intensity with which governesses taught young girls the piano, music, Sebastian had found, was best played when a person had talent. Unfortunately, talent was rather less common than piano lessons.

He braced himself for another rendition of Chopin and pondered whether he might easily sneak from the drawing room. He turned his head but immediately met with a frown from Percival. *Damnation.* Since when did Percival go about glowering at him?

Then he remembered that Leonora was here. His heart swelled for some indiscernible reason.

"Miss Holt, you must play us something," Sebastian said.

Timothy's eyes widened. "Good idea."

Leonora glanced toward the grand piano. "Very well."

"She'll need someone to help her turn the pages." Timothy glanced at Lord Knightley.

Lord Knightley gave a beatific smile. *Mighty Poseidon.* What had compelled Sebastian to invite the man here?

Sebastian shifted his weight from one leg to the other, though he doubted that even sitting in a fluffy armchair with new feathers and expertly fastened horsehair would relieve him of the discomfort he now experienced.

"You'll have to tell me when you need them flipped, Miss Holt," Lord Knightley said.

"I'll help you turn the pages," Sebastian said quickly.

Percival and Cornelius gave him curious glances, but Sebastian gave a bland smile.

"Page turning is an activity greatly assisted by the skill of reading music," Sebastian said. "Nothing worse than fumbled pages in the middle of a superb melody."

Percival and Cornelius nodded.

"You know how to read pages, Your Grace?" Constance asked.

"I do," Sebastian said simply and joined Leonora at the piano.

Certainly Sebastian wasn't volunteering his services for another reason. That would be absurd. The kiss in the music room had been accidental, after all.

Still, when Sebastian stood beside Leonora and her lovely rose scent wafted about him, he was supremely sure he'd made the right choice to volunteer.

Lord Knightley was all the way on the other side of the room, and Sebastian had to restrain himself from grinning too widely.

Leonora began to play. For a moment, Sebastian was transfixed by the rapidity with which her fingers moved from key to key. Her fingers were long and slender, just like she was. Though she seemed restrained, chattering less than her younger sister, Sabrina, the energy that pulsated through her was tangible.

Sebastian turned the pages at the appropriate times, conscious of the magnificent swell of her bosom. He gave a silent prayer of thanks that fichus were not required attire at dinner.

Leonora played multiple pieces, then the room applauded.

He grinned down at her. "You played immaculately."

She smiled back and him, her cheeks a delightful rosy color that matched some of the flowers the gardener might take particular pride in.

"I THINK THAT'S sufficient music," Timothy said suddenly, and Leonora withdrew her hands from the piano.

Constance wrinkled her brow. "Indeed?"

"Yes." Timothy shifted his legs guiltily. "I—er—thought we might like to talk."

"Oh." Constance blinked.

Sabrina raised her handkerchief to her lips. Leonora was fairly certain her sister was smiling. Neither Timothy nor Constance was prone to chatter, lauding the wonders of a peaceful home above all else.

"Is there something in particular you would like to discuss?" Constance asked. The bewilderment in her voice was impossible to ignore.

"Er—"

Julius cleared his throat.

"Yes?" Timothy asked.

Mama gave a pleased smile. Timothy had always been wary of Mama and her lover, but ever since they'd spent more time with each other, Timothy had begun speaking with Julius more and more.

"You forget you are in the presence of a genius," Julius declared.

Leonora's eyes drifted toward Sebastian.

"Indeed?" Timothy asked.

Julius cleared his throat. "I am of course referring to myself."

"N-Naturally," Timothy stammered.

Julius gave Timothy a stern glance. "I have been crowned best artist by *multiple* societies."

"Is there an actual crown involved for those things?" Lord Knightley mused.

Julius flushed. "Of course not. That would be vulgar."

This time, Leonora lifted her handkerchief to her mouth. She was fairly certain Julius would not mind being bestowed with an actual crown.

Lord Knightley turned to Mama. "Tell me, Mrs. Holt, why did you choose to model for Julius? Specifically in that—er—manner?"

Timothy's face reddened, and he opened and shut his mouth several times, as if to contemplate how he might best deter the viscount from this particular conversation topic. Evidently the attempt was doomed, for he remained silent.

"I think it is important to be aware of one's figure," Mama said. "And my portrait did look lovely."

"That is an understatement, and not only because of my immense skills with the brush," Julius said in an unusual display of gallantry.

"What I saw was divine," Lord Knightley said.

Timothy swallowed hard, and he wouldn't have looked out of place on a ship during a storm. "I wasn't aware you had—er—seen the paintings."

Lord Knightley managed to look embarrassed. "Well. Just briefly, of course. I attended Lord and Lady Richmond's ball at the beginning of the season."

"I see," Timothy said with a tight voice. "I wonder if it is appropriate for you to be here."

Lord Knightley's eyes widened. "Excuse me?"

Constance shook her head frantically, and Timothy's shoulders slumped.

"I—er—said, how appropriate it is that you can be here."

Lord Knightley eyed Timothy in stony silence.

"So you can meet Julius," Timothy continued, barreling forward with his lie.

"That is very appropriate," Julius said, smoothing his cravat. "Not everybody who sees my work has the good fortune to spend time with me in a private setting."

Lord Knightley appeared mollified.

Leonora, however, was less pleased. She didn't like the prospect of being married off to someone who enjoyed Julius's paintings of her mother, especially when he was closer to her mother's age than to hers.

She yawned. "I should go to bed."

Then, before anyone could protest, she left the drawing room and marched upstairs.

Unfortunately, even after her maid had helped her undress and Leonora had sunk into the bed, she found sleep elusive. She kept on thinking about her encounter with Sebastian in the library. Her body tingled curiously, and her core tightened.

The down comforter was suddenly too heavy. The air was hot and sticky. It was the sort of weather that everyone spent the whole year yearning for, but now that it was here, it seemed suddenly uncomfortable.

Leonora opened the window. A gentle breeze drifted into the room, thick with the aroma of the floral garden. Moonbeams emitted a silver glow, casting the world in an ethereal light when it was possible to distinguish anything at all.

Leonora returned to the bed. That strange energy still moved through her. The buds of her bosom hardened, and she tentatively snuck her hand toward them, noting the odd manner in which they pebbled.

The evening's conversation entered her mind. She'd never actually examined her body before. When she was naked, it was always in front of a maid or in a bathtub. Perhaps she could examine her body. Was it odd that she'd never done so before?

Leonora lit the candle on her nightstand and crawled from

the bed. She glanced at the window. The curtain was drawn, though a soft breeze came into the room.

Sebastian's manor house was so large that she hadn't needed to share a room with anyone. Leonora stood before the heavy silver mirror in the room and contemplated her reflection.

Chapter Ten

Damnation.

Sebastian stared at the open window.

That was Leonora. Her hair cascaded over her shoulders in a most delicious manner. She no longer wore her customary tight updo that had been wrangled into position by her family's lady's maid. Now her hair was loose and wild. Though the light hindered him from being able to see the color, he knew it was red. He knew it was glossy. A definite urge to touch her silky strands swept through him.

Leonora had abandoned her down comforter, and her figure was clearly visible in the moonlight and the flickering candlelight in her room. Did she not know he could see her? But why would she think someone was strolling outside her window?

He hadn't been able to sleep.

That had been the reason.

Now he definitely would not be able to sleep. Leonora's curved form stood before him, the shape of her bosom clearly visible through her night rail. The thin, gauzy fabric should be illegal. Her alabaster skin glowed under the golden firelight.

He needed to continue walking. He needed to leave this area. And yet…

His eyes continued to be focused on Leonora, and her hand slid toward her night rail.

Mighty Poseidon.

What was she doing?

She was probably changing her clothing. Sebastian didn't go about switching out his nightshirt during the night, but perhaps women were in possession of so many clothes and had such affection for all of them that they thought it necessary to switch from night rail to night rail, just as they switched from morning dress to afternoon dress to evening dress during the day.

He craned his neck and stepped toward the window.

Crack.

It was only a twig, but the sound roared with the efficiency of any lion.

Leonora's eyes widened in the mirror, and for a horrible moment, Sebastian thought she'd seen him.

Sebastian needed to leave. He wasn't supposed to be here. She couldn't find him. Still, he remained transfixed.

⇶⇷

Leonora spotted something in her mirror. Was it an animal? Perhaps a squirrel or hedgehog? She focused on the reflection.

Heavens.

Someone was crouching outside her window.

Leonora stiffened. A jolt of fear moved through her body, then she recognized Sebastian.

She'd memorized the man's sturdy features and jaw long ago.

Her throat dried. What was he doing here?

The curtains were thin, and the wind wafted through the now open window with more force than she'd anticipated. Leonora raised her night rail hastily to her body. The one time she was in a state of undress, someone had seen her.

Sebastian had seen her. And he wasn't moving.

Though Leonora knew she should be appalled, an odd sensation moved through her body. The space between her legs dampened, and the peaks of her bosom hardened.

An odd sensation moved through her. Sebastian was watching. He found this…intriguing. He found *her* intriguing.

She should leap into the bed and perhaps even scream.

And yet…

The very fact Sebastian was watching seemed to usher heat into the room. Her body, certainly, warmed. Her legs became grounded, as if they'd decided they were supposed to be in front of this mirror.

At least, as long as he was watching.

Her heartbeat quickened.

Leonora slid her night rail down slowly. Her skin prickled. Her bodice was bare. She glanced in the mirror, noticing that Sebastian had not disappeared.

Excitement thrummed through her, and she moved the night rail further down. Her breasts were visible. She traced a finger over a breast.

This was the most improper thing Leonora had ever done in her life.

Nothing was more scandalous.

She needed to put her night rail back on at once.

And yet…

For some odd reason, she shifted it lower. Her heart raced as she did so, and the space between her legs ached. She was conscious of Sebastian's large, wide-set eyes, his strong jaw, and his solemn face. His lips were full and appealing, and memories of their kiss today filled her mind. Her lips had sought his unconsciously, and the experience had been more pleasurable than anything she could have imagined.

Even though this was terribly naughty, Leonora dropped her night rail.

⊱⋅ ──── ⋅⊰

MIGHTY POSEIDON.

Leonora was nude. Pink peaks crowned her high breasts. Her

waist was narrow, and her hips slipped out in an interesting manner. She was slender, resembling a fairy queen.

Sebastian's heartbeat quickened, and the world felt hot and sticky. His breath sauntered away from him, and his cock hardened.

He backed away quickly. Unfortunately, he collided with something solid, and in the moment after that, he toppled backward into a bush. Branches broke and poked his skin, and a distinct floral scent wafted about him.

Blast.

He'd crashed into the lilacs.

Sebastian bit his lip, managing to restrain himself from uttering an ungentlemanly curse, or worse, an ungentlemanly yelp. His heroism was evidently not successful.

Leonora flung on a robe and ducked her head from the window. "What happened?"

Sebastian was very, very still.

He was *not* going to be caught outside Leonora's window at this time of night. He willed himself to blend into the lilac bush and glowered at the offending tree root that had sent him barreling onto the ground.

The tree remained lofty and unmoving, just as it always did. If it had a face, no doubt it would have smirked.

Leonora continued to survey the outside.

Please don't let her notice me. Please don't let her notice me. Please don't let her notice me.

"Sebastian?" Leonora's alto voice was unmistakable.

Sebastian remained silent. Perhaps Leonora could be convinced she was simply imagining his presence.

Yes. That was the best plan: immobility.

"Sebastian. I see you," Leonora said sternly. "Are you injured?"

"Just a bruise."

"G-Good." Leonora nodded rapidly. Her cheeks were flushed. "Why were you there?"

Sebastian raised his chin defiantly. "I was going on a walk."

"Outside my window?"

"Outside all the windows."

Leonora blinked.

"That came out poorly," Sebastian said hastily. "As if I made a point of walking outside people's bedroom windows on purpose. I—er—just meant I often take a walk at night. I didn't expect to s—"

Her eyes widened.

"Not that I saw anything," Sebastian blurted. Fire burned the back of his neck, as if he'd fallen onto a hearth and not a bush. He resisted the temptation to dab his nape like a madman.

"Oh." Leonora averted her gaze.

Sebastian frowned. Why was Leonora staring at the carpet? If she should be staring at anything, it should be the lilac bush that had felled him. Clearly the bush's branches had simply become far too long and his gardeners' performance was exemplary. Overexemplary, in fact, given the magnificent state of the bush.

Was it possible she'd seen him? Before he'd fallen? After all, she had said his name at once. Surely she couldn't automatically attribute each crunch of branches to him?

The sound of a sash window sliding open filled the air, and Sebastian froze.

Someone had heard something.

Blast.

He was *not* going to be discovered talking to Leonora through an open window late at night. That was the sort of thing that would spark gossip, and Sebastian was in no mood for anyone to speak about them with glinting eyes and smirks, hinting at weddings and the loveliness of their future babies were they to mate.

That was the sort of thing he did not desire at all.

Sebastian didn't think.

Instead, he charged toward Leonora's window and scrambled inside.

Leonora's blue eyes widened, and her long lashes darted up. "What—?"

Sebastian put his hand over Leonora's mouth before she could utter anything else. Unfortunately, he only noted the lushness of Leonora's full lips. Why on earth did they need to be so perfectly shaped? She may as well have been wickedness itself.

Sebastian remembered that Leonora's window was open and shut it rapidly. Then he closed the curtain.

"Why are you here?" Leonora whispered.

"So I am not caught talking to you at a late hour," Sebastian whispered equally harshly.

Didn't she understand?

"Surely the concept is not difficult to grasp," he added.

Irritation moved over Leonora's exquisite face. "I wouldn't have thought entering my room was the best way to avoid being seen with me."

He arched an eyebrow. "Are you going to tell anyone?" He smirked. "You're not trying to trap me into marriage?"

"I would never want to be married to you," she said firmly. "You're appalling."

Sebastian's chest tightened. Leonora's words shouldn't have felt injurious, and yet, for an odd moment, she may as well have been wielding a battle-ax.

"Am I?" He narrowed the distance between them.

He knew he should hurry from the room. He didn't want to be discovered in this corridor.

But something about her drove him mad. The candlelight flickered over her delicate skin, dancing among her freckles.

He caught her rosy lips with his and pulled her toward him.

It was just a kiss.

He'd kissed dozens of women before. In fact, he'd even kissed Leonora before.

It was just a kiss, then he could leave.

He hadn't planned for his heart to pound at the sensation of her lips. Her bosom pressed against his chest in a most fascinating manner, now unconstrained by any corset or shift. Her soft mounds prompted him to moan.

Her body relaxed against him, and her arms wrapped around his chest.

He should let go.

He should apologize.

But instead, he grasped her more tightly to him and continued to kiss her.

This felt excellent. Most magnificent.

His cock hardened and pointed toward the ceiling. His breeches had never felt so uncomfortable.

Fire moved through him. The air was thick and dewy. He continued to kiss and kiss and kiss Leonora.

If he opened his eyes, if he released her, he would have to pretend this had been a mistake. He would have to leave the room.

He didn't want to do that.

He only desired to test her. He only desired to feel the delicious curves of her tall, slender form.

He only wanted…her.

Had he craved her in London? He wasn't certain. Perhaps that energy had always existed between them, crackling and swaying.

Reluctantly he pulled himself from her.

"I shouldn't have done that," he said, his voice hoarse.

"No," she said, her eyes still on him.

"I should go," he said.

"Yes," she agreed.

Sebastian didn't move.

He couldn't move.

His legs seemed to scoff at the idea of walking, as if they hadn't been created to step away from her.

"I should go," he said finally, his voice hoarse.

She nodded silently, her eyes still wide, and Sebastian hurried into the corridor.

Chapter Eleven

Sebastian opened the door to his room. He didn't bother to light the conveniently placed candle, as if he could swathe himself in the room's darkness.

Perhaps then he could forget Leonora.

He moved gingerly over the wooden floorboards and the various aesthetically placed Persian carpets. Though the rugs were useful when he was barefoot, they were rather less convenient now he was making his way through to a dark room.

He stumbled into his quarters, then flung himself onto his bed. He tore off his shoes and tossed them to the side. He slid off his trousers, grateful his valet had already retired for the night, then removed his shirt.

The sheets were soft, and energy swirled through him. His cock remained stiff.

Mighty Poseidon.

Sebastian longed to take his cock into his hand.

I am not thinking of Leonora.

He was desperate for release. If he moved his fingers over his cock, it would be something mechanical, nothing more. He would just be checking that everything was working correctly. A health check.

Except most health checks didn't take place after midnight. Visions of Leonora filled his mind. Visions of her smooth skin.

Her rounded form. The exact curve of her bottom, the exact narrowness of her waist, and the glimpse of her rounded bosom were seared on his mind.

She was heavenly.

Even though she was absolutely not supposed to be.

He wasn't thinking of her. He wasn't thinking of her auburn hair and her wide-set eyes. He certainly wasn't thinking of her luscious lips and remembering how they felt against his own.

Sebastian moved his hand down the muscular planes of his chest, then brushed his fingers against his cock.

It was only coincidence it had decided tonight to stand straight up and adopt rocklike properties.

It was not because he'd encountered Leonora. *Nude.*

The memory of her caused his cock to swell even more.

He needed release. He craved it.

Blast.

Sebastian took his cock in his hand. The tip was already moist, and he ran his fingers down the length. He groaned, then bit his lip hard.

Perhaps if he could finish hastily, he could avoid thinking any more of Leonora.

He flung his coverlet from him, and the air wafted about him. He moved his fist hastily up and down his length. Pleasure shot through him, and he quickened his speed.

Images of Leonora entered his mind, but he shut his eyes firmly, as if that could possibly erase her image.

Unfortunately, it did no such thing.

He forced himself to think of other women. He wasn't a virgin. There were widows. Women whom everyone agreed were paragons of beauty.

And yet Leonora danced upon his mind. Something about her filled him with lust.

His hand moved quickly, quickly, quickly.

A sweaty scent wafted to his nostrils, but he continued.

What would it be like to touch Leonora? To hold her in his

arms? To run his fingers along her satin skin? Every curve seemed enticing.

Leonora was regal and aloof. She was a queen.

A duchess.

Sebastian forced that thought away. He wasn't going to think about a world where Leonora was beside him all the time. That was sentimental soppiness.

Instead, he gave in to imageries of kissing her again. Of sucking on her skin. Of claiming her body.

He wanted to memorize every curve with his tongue and lips. He wanted to explore the underside of her ears, and he wanted to taste the delicate skin of her neck.

He yearned for her.

What would it be like to delve into her silky folds? To push into pure bliss? Would her cheeks darken with pleasure? Would she scream?

Energy pulsed through him. His cock throbbed and jerked.

Sebastian firmed his grip on it, moving faster and faster and faster.

In the next moment, his seed spurted, and a masculine aroma spread over the bed.

Tiredness moved through him, melded with another sensation…shame.

He yanked the blanket over him, willing himself to sleep.

⇶⇷

LIGHT CASCADED THROUGH the room.

"Good morning, Your Grace," his valet said cheerfully.

His eyes were still thick with sleep, and Sebastian brushed away the sand.

"Good morning, Robert," Sebastian said.

A fire danced in the hearth. How long had he been sleeping? He scrambled into a sitting position. Someone had put a silver platter of tea, milk, and breakfast delicacies on his side table.

"What time is it?"

"Late," Robert said casually, then his eyes narrowed. "Are those your clothes?"

Robert immediately clamped his mouth shut, and Sebastian's face flamed.

Sebastian's clothes were lying in an undignified pile.

"I redressed to take a walk last night," Sebastian said.

"Ah." Robert nodded. "You could have woken me up. I could have helped you."

"I managed," Sebastian said stiffly.

Robert nodded and picked up the discarded shirt and trousers from the floor.

Sebastian drank a long sip of tea, ignoring the fact it was still hot and that he had yet to put milk in it.

"I thought you would prefer to have breakfast in your room," Robert said.

"Very considerate of you." Sebastian nodded. "But—I—should go greet everyone."

"Indeed, Your Grace?" Robert raised an eyebrow.

"It is not every day my house is filled with guests, Robert."

It certainly wasn't every day one of his guests was Leonora.

Chapter Twelve

Leonora wandered into the wooded area behind the house. Large trees loomed above her, and wildflowers dotted the ground in the spaces where the sunlight touched. Leonora stomped further into the woods, until the trees obscured the castle entirely. Wildflowers jutted out their vibrant heads, and birds chirped from above.

Where was the lake?

"Leonora?" came a surprised voice.

She drew back.

"Good morning." Leonora curtsied and shot Sebastian her best nonchalant nod and pretended he had not seen her naked the night before.

Sebastian gazed at her with an amused expression. "What are you doing here?"

She lifted her chin. "Exploring."

"In that dress?" He raised an eyebrow.

"I am not equipped with boots and buckskin breeches."

"Of course not," he said. "I'm sorry."

The silence filled the room with the sort of discomfort she'd only read about. She could hear each leaf rustle and each twig crack. The latter sound made her remember last night, and her heartbeat quickened.

"Perhaps since you are already—er—outside, you would care

to join me on a walk," Sebastian said.

"A walk?" Leonora's voice squeaked uncharacteristically, but Sebastian appeared unfazed.

Sebastian nodded. "Indeed. There are some rose gardens that are apparently worthy of attention."

She stared at him.

"Should you interest yourself in horticulture," he added. "Or—er—botany."

"I do find flowers pretty," she admitted.

"Ah." His shoulders eased.

Had he truly been nervous before? Leonora narrowed her eyes.

"I won't harm you," he promised.

Leonora drew back. "I rather assumed you wouldn't."

"O-Of course." For a moment, Sebastian seemed uncertain, and she was reminded of the boy he'd once been.

The boy alone on the large estate on the other side of the trees.

The boy who would sneak out and play with her every day after his tutoring lessons.

The boy whose parents she never saw and whose tutors were all uniformly frightening.

"Very well," Leonora said briskly. "Let's go."

Sebastian nodded. He glanced at the sky. "Though, it is drizzling now."

"Well, we wouldn't want that to turn to a downpour. And we are already outside."

"Indeed." Sebastian's demeanor lacked its customary confidence, but they started to stroll together.

"I didn't know you wrote music," Leonora said.

Sebastian opened his mouth, then shut it.

Leonora tilted her head at him. "Will you deny it?"

His cheeks grew a ruddy color, then he shook his head.

"I knew it," she said triumphantly. "Though, I never would have suspected."

Sebastian's lips twitched. "Well, I didn't write music when I was ten years old. Unlike Mozart, I didn't start learning music until the utterly advanced age of eleven."

"Well, you are quite wonderful," Leonora said.

Sebastian smirked. "You're correct."

"At least, I was enjoying your composition until you took it away."

"Actually, you gave me the idea to take music," Sebastian confessed.

Leonora's eyes widened.

"I remember how fond you always were of playing the piano, and you used to talk about it. I don't think I ever heard you play though. But…" He bit his lip. "When everything changed, I had more time, and I asked for lessons."

"Oh. I didn't know that."

He smiled, and they continued to stroll through the wooded area. The conversation was supposed to be awkward and terrible. And yet everything was pleasant. She was reminded of when he'd simply been her next-door neighbor, the boy whom she'd confided in about everything. Except now things were difficult. Now Sebastian was grown.

Sebastian's brandy-and-citrus scent wafted about her, more delicious than any compilation the forest could conjure. She fought the urge to inhale and bit her lip.

She had the horrible thought he was not nearly as dreadful as she'd always thought. Worse, it occurred to her that she might even care for him. She was supposed to care for her future husband, whomever that might be.

She wasn't supposed to think about Sebastian. She certainly was not supposed to contemplate the man's broad shoulders, glittering dark eyes, and long lashes. She wasn't going to think about the man's handsome features.

It didn't help he shared her passion for music.

"Your father must have been proud of your music," she said, remembering how close Sebastian and his father had been.

Sebastian gave a wry smile. "I don't think Father was particularly impressed by the fact I desired lessons. He didn't want to have a weak son, and music, well…"

"He thought music was something for women to do?" Leonora said.

"Precisely."

"I can assure you not every woman is musical."

"No." Sebastian shook his head. "Perhaps not. Anyway, I started playing the piano, but then because Father didn't like it, I turned to writing the music. I could hear the music in my mind and be quiet. He could think I was doing other things."

"That's very clever of you," Leonora said.

Sebastian gave a boastful shrug. "Indeed."

"But your music is incredible. Just the ability to compose any music is incredible, but this…" Leonora sighed. "How did I not know that?"

"You don't know everything," Sebastian said.

"But does anyone else know? Your friends? I thought Percival might have mentioned something."

A funny look passed over Sebastian's face.

"Though, of course they must know. They must just be discreet."

"Neither Percival nor Cornelius knows," Sebastian admitted. "I have some other friends, though, who work with music a lot. They know."

"Oh." Leonora stiffened. The fact shouldn't have been embarrassing for Sebastian, but his face was distinctly redder than before.

"Is that how you know Mimi?" Leonora asked.

Sebastian nodded.

"I thought…" Leonora hesitated. She didn't want to tell him what she'd thought.

"Mimi and I are friends," Sebastian blurted. "That's all we've ever been."

"She spoke highly of you."

"Contrary to your opinion, I'm not completely terrible."

This time, Leonora averted her eyes. "I suppose you're not," she said softly. "I must apologize."

Sebastian took her hands in his. "And I must apologize to you."

She nodded and drew back.

Disappointment flickered over his face. She wanted to explain, but what could she say? That his mere touch made her body tingle in odd ways? Should she tell him that it took effort to not stare at his lips or wonder at the beauty of his eyes?

The thought was impossible, and she folded her hands together.

Sebastian tilted her chin up and gazed down at her. Her heartbeat quickened. His hand was firm and warm. Then Sebastian leaned toward her and kissed her.

This wasn't an accident, not that any kisses could truly be termed accidents.

The woodsy scent filled her nostrils, and her feet crunched over twigs. She stumbled, and he clutched her in his sturdy arms.

He cupped her face in his hands, and a shiver moved through her. The world consisted entirely of him.

His hand brushed against her body, and her blood seemed to rush to meet him. Certainly, the rest of her body felt weak. Her legs wobbled, and her heart bounced up and down uncertainly.

He then removed his lips from hers, and she let out a moan of frustration. He gave her one of those cocky grins that made her chest do odd things, then he pressed his lips to her neck. He trailed kisses toward her bosom, nibbling on the arch of her throat.

This was absolutely forbidden.

Sebastian shouldn't be doing this.

And this certainly shouldn't feel as wonderful as it did.

Leonora's legs wobbled, and she inched toward a tree and leaned against its trunk.

He kissed her cheek, then he kissed her lips.

>>><<<

Damnation.

Kissing Leonora had never been the plan. But now Sebastian couldn't imagine not doing it. The world only consisted of her delicious lips, and her elegant arms, and her curved body.

Dim light shone through the tall trees. He couldn't see Leonora's beautiful freckles, and he couldn't see her skin pinken as he touched her. He brushed his lips against her long neck, enjoying its silky texture, and inhaled her floral scent.

They kissed and kissed, until raindrops fell upon them, and he removed himself from her reluctantly.

Her eyes sparkled. "I suppose we'll have to postpone teaching me how to fish."

He chuckled, and his heart felt light.

Chapter Thirteen

Leonora strolled to the dining room, happy she'd brought her most beautiful gown with her. She wanted to look nice for Sebastian.

She hadn't been able to speak with him all day. Timothy had insisted she sit beside Lord Knightley at lunch, and she was fully prepared to sit with him at dinner as well and make conversation about horticulture. Never mind that horticulture had never intrigued her much in the past, and never mind that she'd much prefer speaking about music with Sebastian.

She was still astounded by the duke's talent. Why on earth did he keep it secret from everyone? And how had he ever managed to do so for so long?

"Miss Holt." Sebastian bowed as she entered the dining room. "You look lovely."

A pleasant warmth spread through her.

Timothy cleared his throat. "Indeed. Don't you think she looks lovely, Lord Knightley?"

"Most certainly," Lord Knightley said quickly.

Timothy hastened to Sebastian. "I was hoping you could tell me about the history of the castle. I'm—er—quite fascinated by it. What architects did your family use?"

"They're dead," Sebastian said flatly. "Just in case you were thinking of stealing them."

Timothy's cheeks turned a ruddy color, and Leonora's eyes narrowed. What exactly had happened between them?

Lord Knightley, though, guided her into the dining room, and she was soon occupied with eating.

Once the dinner ended, Lord Knightley shot her a meaningful look. "Would you like to see the pagoda?"

The man stared at her with such intensity something dropped in Leonora's stomach. Surely he didn't consider himself to be courting her?

But from the eager smiles of her family, Leonora had the horrible sense Lord Knightley was here to do that. Hadn't Mrs. Feldman said her nephew desired to settle down? Precisely how highly had Mrs. Feldman spoken of her? What emotions of pity had Timothy inspired in her?

Perhaps Mrs. Feldman simply wanted all her former students to find husbands, even if it required her charges to marry her own relatives.

Leonora glanced toward her brother. "I don't think it would be proper."

"I don't mind," Timothy announced.

Mama frowned. "But if she doesn't want to go…"

"Nonsense," Timothy said. "Exercise is always good."

"I don't think it's far enough away to count as exercise," Leonora said.

"Well, that settles it," Timothy said. "No reason not to go."

Heavens. Was he *winking* at Lord Knightley?

Lord Knightley extended his arm, and Leonora took it.

Sebastian's face was pale as Lord Knightley ushered her away. Soon the viscount was guiding her outside. The grass was no longer wet from its morning rain shower.

"I take it you are not particularly fond of pagodas, Miss Holt?"

"Not more than most people," she admitted.

"Ah. What do you like, then?"

"Music."

"Ah." Lord Knightley nodded. "Very admirable. Though, I do

find that music interferes with reading, don't you think?"

"I suppose so," Leonora admitted.

Lord Knightley beamed. "Then we are in agreement."

"I wouldn't say—"

In the next moment, Lord Knightley knelt. "Since you're not particularly fond of pagodas, I thought there was no reason to go all the way there."

"Indeed, Lord Knightley?" The horrible feeling in Leonora's chest grew.

"I want to marry you, Miss Holt," Lord Knightley said. "Now, will you be my viscountess?"

"I—"

Lord Knightley cast a glance at the pagoda, perhaps wishing he was not kneeling on the wet grass and had led her to the pagoda after all. "Make me a happy man!"

"But we've just met. You can't already be in love with me."

Lord Knightley blinked. "Love would be hasty." He grinned. "But does that mean you already are in love with me?" He eyed his chest. "Perhaps my heart is beating more rapidly than normal. Is yours?"

"N-No," Leonora said hurriedly, though it occurred to her that her heart *did* beat quite rapidly in Sebastian's presence.

Heavens.

What on earth was she doing outside with Lord Knightley?

"Please get up, Lord Knightley," she said.

"Was that a yes?" he said eagerly.

"No," she said regretfully.

He blinked in obvious confusion. "But you do know I am a viscount?"

"I do," she said.

"And you do know I am offering to make you a viscountess?"

"I do," she said miserably. "But I'm afraid I don't love you."

"Since when is love mandatory? We have years to fall in love. Decades, in fact."

Leonora grimaced. She didn't want to wait decades to fall in love with her husband.

"As nice as that sounds," Leonora said, "I must decline."

"Do you think you'll change your mind?"

She shook her head. "I know you'll make someone a wonderful husband."

"That is hardly comfort now." He hesitated. "Please tell your family and the duke goodbye. I don't think I can bear to meet them now. I will leave."

"I understand," Leonora said, then the viscount headed toward his wing.

Leonora returned to the castle by herself and rejoined her family.

"You're back!" Constance's eyes shone. "Where is the viscount?"

"He's going to leave early."

"Oh." Constance blinked and exchanged a somber glance with Timothy.

"Where is the duke?" Leonora asked, noticing he was absent.

"He retired," Timothy said. "A bit rude, I thought. Would have expected him to want to join in the celebrations."

Leonora's throat dried. "Did you by any chance tell him what Lord Knightley wanted to speak to me about?"

Timothy nodded. "Of course." His eyes narrowed. "Did Lord Knightley—"

"He proposed," Leonora said shortly.

The others looked ready to exclaim joyous expressions.

"But I said no," Leonora said hastily. "I don't want to marry him."

"But he's perfect," Sabrina said with a shocked expression.

"I don't love him."

The room was silent.

"Perhaps you will grow to love him," Constance said finally.

"No." Leonora sighed. "And now I will retire."

Before her family could laud the viscount again, she hurried to her room.

SOMETHING STRUCK THE windowpane, and Sebastian frowned. Had he imagined it? This night was not windy. Had something fallen from the roof, perhaps?

The sound occurred again. This time, Sebastian abandoned the comfort of his bed. It wasn't as if he'd been getting much sleep in it. Contemplating Lord Knightley and Leonora in future wedded bliss was not particularly conducive to sleep.

He moved the heavy jacquard drapes and peered into the midnight sky. The moonlight was not as strong as yesterday, hindered by the clouds that so frequently settled upon British skies even in the height of summer, as if this was their most beloved place to be.

Sebastian stepped onto the balcony. He'd forgotten to put on slippers, and the marble was cold against his feet. A tree obscured part of his view. He thrust his gaze around, half expecting to see part of the castle crumble down. Instead, he saw a figure. A female figure, judging from the attire. Was it...her?

Despite his best efforts to brace himself for disappointment—after all, there was no reason for *her* to be outside his window—his heartbeat quickened.

"Sebastian?" came a whisper.

Now there was no doubt.

It was Leonora. His heart soared, as if one of the eagles that lived on the estate had taken hold of it and was carrying it to the heavens.

Then he remembered that most likely she was here simply to tell him she was now betrothed to Lord Knightley. After all, how long did it take to propose?

"Leonora?" He leaned over the balustrades. "What are you doing there?"

She hurried toward him. "I needed to speak with you." She surveyed the balcony. "I assume there's a way up?"

He blinked. "The servants keep ladders somewhere. But I can come down…"

"No matter," Leonora chirped.

In the next moment, she took hold of the tree and pulled herself up onto a branch.

"You mustn't," Sebastian said, and his heart lurched in his chest. "You might hurt yourself."

"Have you forgotten all the trees we used to climb, Your Grace?" Leonora popped her head over the balustrade, and her lips opened into a grin.

Sebastian chuckled and pulled her onto the balcony. "No, I don't command such powers of memory loss."

"Indeed."

"Nor would I want to," he said, and his voice was hoarse, as if squeezed by the wild thumping of his heart.

Leonora's smile disappeared, and he was suddenly aware of the narrowness of her shoulders and the fact she was trembling.

"You're cold," he said.

"No," she said. "But I do need to tell you something."

"You better come inside," Sebastian said, his voice more solemn. "I know about the proposal."

"I know," she said.

Well.

That was that. She was officially betrothed. He suspected most women did not celebrate the joining of their hearts with other men by throwing stones at balcony windows and pulling themselves up, but Leonora was not most women.

He averted his gaze, focusing on lighting the candle by the balcony door. The room was soon swathed in soft light he immediately regretted, lest Leonora see the somber expression on his face.

It shouldn't have mattered if she was now engaged to Lord Knightley, but his heart ached. He inclined his head into a nod and forced his lips into a stiff smile. "Please let me extend my fondest congratulations."

The effort shouldn't have been difficult. Murmuring congratulations to people was one of the most frequent social demands he was asked to perform, and he would always have termed it the easiest. Certainly he had ample opportunity to practice. Many gatherings were centered around occasions in which the hosts demanded felicitations: weddings, betrothals, baptisms.

"I-I told him no," Leonora blurted.

Sebastian widened his eyes. "I don't understand."

Lord Knightley was an ideal match. The viscount had an agreeable disposition, and he'd never outgrown his cherubic features.

"I shouldn't have come here," Leonora said. "I just wanted you to know. That's all." She took a deep breath, as if she was also suffering the rapidly beating heart syndrome that had recently affected him. "I-I would want to know."

In the next moment, she turned back toward the balcony door.

"Wait!" Sebastian extended an arm, touching her shoulder. "Don't leave."

She stilled, and her delightful rose scent wafted about him.

"I did want to know," he admitted, his voice hoarse.

"You did?" she breathed.

"Indeed." He moved her body around tentatively, conscious of the way in which the candlelight flickered over her delicate skin, illuminating her in a glittering golden glow.

He moved closer to her, as if she was a prized painting in a gallery. "I don't want to argue anymore."

"I don't either," she said softly, and something in his chest panged.

In the next moment, he caught her lips in his own, and everything was blissful. His heart thumped madly against his ribs.

"I thought I'd lost you," he murmured.

She gave him a wry smile. "Perhaps I'm not so easy to lose."

"No." He pulled her tightly to him, encircling her waist with his arms. "You most decidedly are not." He kissed the thin skin that led to her ear. "I was a fool to ever desire that."

"Indeed?" Her voice wobbled.

"Most decidedly. I hope you can forgive me."

She gave him a beatific smile, and warmth surged through him. How odd that he'd dreaded this house party, dreaded her arrival even in London.

"I think I was waiting to see you again for a very long time." He trailed his hands over her slender body, indulging in each curve. Her bottom rounded in a most captivating way, and he devoted particular attention to that region. He pressed his lips against her earlobe, then caught it in his mouth.

Leonora gasped.

How odd that he'd spent so much time on music when the sweetest sound in the world was that of Leonora's moans. He removed the pins from her updo, and her long locks tumbled into his hands.

He moved his fingers to her bosom, removed her fichu, and flung it on the opposite side of the bedroom. Then he focused on her dress. Though it might have some fashionable merits as well, right now he wanted Leonora to be naked. He wanted to feel her soft skin. Shifts and stays were things to despise.

Finally, he removed all her clothes and laid her on the bed. The candlelight flickered over her skin.

"I want to kiss every inch of you," he murmured.

"Then do it," Leonora said.

"You mean it?"

"Naturally." She smiled, and he crawled onto the mattress quickly, not minding that the bed cords sagged. It only meant he was even closer to Leonora.

Her bare bosom pressed against his, and he bent down to capture her rosy peaks in his mouth.

Leonora moaned and writhed.

"Was that fine?" he asked, suddenly worried.

"No."

Oh.

He stiffened.

Leonora picked up a pillow and flung it at Sebastian's face.

"That was wonderful!" she exclaimed, and he grinned.

"I despise you," he murmured.

She laughed happily.

Perhaps this was what it was like to fall in love with one's dearest friend. Even though they hadn't seen each other for years, that was what she was. That was what she'd always been.

What she always would be.

His cock ached, and she reached for it tentatively.

"May I touch it?" she asked.

"You may," he said, his voice hoarse. Apparently his heart had decided it was impossible for it to beat wildly and him to speak articulately at the same time.

In the next moment, Leonora's slender hands were upon his cock. She stroked it. "Does that feel good?"

He nodded, wide-eyed. "How did you—"

"I do have two sisters," Leonora said. "And one of them is married." She frowned. "Though, my younger sister does seem suspiciously well acquainted with a man's anatomy."

He chuckled. "Perhaps that comes from designing clothes."

"Perhaps," Leonora said uncertainly.

"What else did your sisters talk about?"

"They said the most satisfaction comes when a man's cock is inserted inside a woman."

He grinned. "You have very intelligent sisters."

"That's what they always say."

He laughed despite himself. Bedding a woman wasn't supposed to be so delightful, but there was no other way to describe what was happening now.

Leonora wrinkled her brow. "Should I simply mount it?"

"You could. Though, I suggest we use a French sleeve first." He climbed off the bed, found a French sleeve, and put it on his cock.

Leonora stared at it curiously. "Is it ready now?"

"Indeed," Sebastian said.

In the next moment, Leonora straddled him and lowered herself slowly onto his cock.

He grunted.

"Was that—"

"That was bloody fantastic," he muttered.

She grinned. "No pillow flinging first?"

"No," he said. "Just continue."

And they did.

Leonora moved up and down his cock. Her breasts bounced appealingly. He shouldn't have been surprised Leonora would be forward in the bedroom. She was strong and determined and the most wonderful woman he'd ever met.

He moved his hands to her bottom.

"That's nice," she murmured, her breath less steady than normal.

Finally, Leonora moaned and moaned and arched her back up.

Sebastian's world exploded, and he collapsed on top of her. "My love."

They lay naked beside each other, and Sebastian drew her to him. He kissed her cheeks, her earlobes, her neck, and that interesting area where her bodice met her bosom. Leonora moaned in his arms, and everything was wonderful.

"I love you," Sebastian said, and his heart quaked.

He'd never said those words to anyone. He didn't think he'd even said them to his parents. And yet, at the moment, he knew they were absolutely true. He loved Leonora. He adored her. She was everything. He pulled her tighter, as if the mere action of touching her, of having her skin press against his, might reassure him of the reality of her existence. Even that seemed incredible.

She turned her neck to him and stared at him, and his heart caught as he gazed into her beautiful eyes.

"You do?" she murmured.

For a horrible, panicky moment, Sebastian thought she would

only find his statement amusing. After all, wasn't he supposed to hate her? Hadn't that been something he'd stated, multiple times, to almost anyone who would listen? Certainly his friends would have said he despised her. In fact, they also would have said she despised him.

Over a moment, the room became chillier, then he inhaled and nodded solemnly.

"I do," he said.

It didn't matter if she didn't love him. She simply needed to know he loved her and that she was so immensely wondrous. She needed to know she made his heart sing in a manner nothing else in the world had made it do before. She needed to know her very existence, the fact the world had somehow created someone so incredible as her—that that alone brought joy to him.

"You don't have to say anything," he said. "I merely wanted you to know."

She continued to stare at him.

Heavens, he could get lost in her eyes. Her lashes were so long and that color gleamed with such force that it was a wonder she had not instantly been crowned the most beautiful woman in London the moment she had set foot in the capital.

This manor house should be swarming with suitors for her. In fact, if anyone in London had any sense, they would be vying for her hand immediately, and he would be there fighting for her.

Heavens, if this were the Middle Ages, he would be fighting for her with sword in hand, eager to show his prowess to her in any battle or game that she could imagine. Win at jousting? He would do that, if it meant her. Win at swordsmanship? Oh yes, he could do that too. Fight a dragon? He would be first in line, if only it meant she would wear his colors.

He pressed his lips against her skin, now sticky from their activity. Her delicious scent, stronger now, floated over him. He wished it were morning and he could see the sunbeams play along her delightful skin. Even though the drapes were shut, he had limited himself to a single candle, lest any servant notice the light and wonder why he was still awake.

Leonora wasn't supposed to be here. She wasn't supposed to be lying in his arms, and he wasn't supposed to be saying such words to her.

In fact, he would have been the first man to tease someone who acted like him, and yet everything he'd told her was the truth. His heart thrummed. Even if he didn't know what would happen in the future, he did know he loved her. And in some manner, that was enough.

"I wish we'd never stopped speaking," he said.

"I wish the same."

"I wish our fathers had never fought."

She nodded. "I do too."

Sebastian kissed Leonora's forehead, and warmth surged through him.

He wanted to take care of her for the rest of his life.

He smiled as he pulled her slip over her.

The door opened, and Sabrina barged in. Her eyes widened, and her mouth gaped. "I didn't think you would go through with your asinine plan."

Leonora froze in Sebastian's arms, as if she'd suddenly been turned to stone.

CHAPTER FOURTEEN

SABRINA'S WORDS SURGED through Sebastian's mind with the force of the most powerful opera singer's vocal cords. Nothing had been real.

His heart shattered. Leonora had concocted some sort of plan that involved them being together in an amorous state. Leonora had only pretended to care for him. Sebastian should have known better.

Had she been hoping for her brother to happen upon them and insist on a wedding so she might become a duchess? Or had she hoped simply to toy with his emotions?

The air was utterly still, and Leonora's cheeks grew a horrible white color. She turned to her sister and shook her head.

Her sister stepped back. "I'm sorry. I suppose I shouldn't have said that."

"No," Leonora said, "you shouldn't have."

Sebastian rose. He didn't want to hear Leonora chide her sister that she had made Leonora's despicable plan evident.

"You needn't worry, Sabrina," he said icily. "I'm glad I know."

Leonora quivered, and Sebastian wished he could take pleasure from her distress. The world wobbled as if he was trapped on a ship during a terrible storm, and he clutched hold of a nearby armchair. He gripped it with such force the whites of his knuckles were visible under the strange, fluttering light of Sabrina's lantern.

"Is it true?" He articulated each word slowly.

She nodded finally. "But you don't understand. I…"

"You what?"

She bit her lips and was silent. Finally, she said, "That was before I knew you."

He turned around impatiently, then shot a glance back at her. "You've known me since we were children."

"I know, but things were different."

"What was different? You enjoyed yourself? You hoped for more such occasions?"

Dread crept into Sebastian's stomach, and his voice sounded harsh. "Please leave us, Miss Holt. Leonora and I have something important to discuss."

The door closed behind Sabrina, and Sebastian glared. "This was a plan? A trick? A trap? To what end?"

Leonora finally moved, but her voice sounded distant. "You don't understand."

"Enlighten me, then."

Leonora's face remained white. "I was going to trap you into a compromising position to ruin your reputation."

Sebastian stiffened.

He'd been expecting her to say she desired marriage. Other debutantes desired that as well. But instead, she'd wanted to harm and disgrace him. Everything between them had been a lie.

"That's why you hired Mimi," Sebastian said.

Leonora gave a miserable nod.

"I asked if you had anything to do with it." Sebastian stared at her. "You told me you didn't know her. You lied."

Leonora drew back. "I know."

"You should have told me," he said.

"I know," she agreed. "I'm sorry."

"That's not enough."

"I know. I really am so sorry. I should explain."

"There's nothing else you can say," Sebastian said flatly. "I see I've made a horrible mistake. Under the circumstances, you'll understand why I don't offer for you. If anyone asks for me, you can kindly tell them I've returned to my own estate."

Without another word or backward glance, he stormed from his room. He marched faster and faster until he reached the staircase.

He hurried over the marble tiles that had gleamed so beautifully in the light but were now simply slippery places to be injured.

He'd been fooled, just like his father had been fooled. He'd trusted Leonora, just like his father had trusted Leonora's father.

Sebastian hadn't learned anything. Heavens, he'd given his heart to her. He'd been so foolish.

He opened the door, then hurried outside. He didn't care much for waking up his driver, but he needed to leave immediately. He needed to be as far from here as possible.

Sebastian quickened his stride and cut across the meadow, toward the stables. His feet trampled over the long strands of grass, places the sheep had not yet had time to graze. Stars lit the sky, shimmering like diamonds, as if this was possibly a night to celebrate.

He entered the stables. Warmth filled the windowless building, and his feet crunched over the hay. Where was Bates?

"Your Grace?" his groom asked in a startled manner.

"Ah, yes," Sebastian said. "Bates, I was hoping we could leave."

"Indeed?"

Sebastian nodded. "We can stop at the next public house. I don't want to be here."

"Very well." Bates avoided Sebastian's gaze. "I shall prepare the horses."

"Better get a servant to gather my things."

"Yes, Your Grace."

Sebastian sat in his carriage and scowled.

He'd had all the knowledge to prepare himself, yet somehow, he'd managed to make a mess of everything.

He'd been so foolish.

Would Leonora continue to appear in his dreams for the rest of his life, before he woke up and remembered everything between them had been false? Would he have to scurry from balls in which she appeared on the arm of some aristocrat she deemed superior?

Sebastian pressed his lips together. That was a question for the future. Currently, the only question was how to put as much distance between him and her as possible.

The horses moved languidly over the road, hampered by the dim light, despite the lack of other carriages on the roads. The outline of the castle mocked him in the distance.

This was his home, yet now it was forever tainted.

Chapter Fifteen

Leonora picked up her skirts and hurried past Sebastian's family portraits, past the antique sideboards and chairs, and past the glossy oriental vases, now only dim shadows.

Finally, she entered her bedroom. She shut her door hastily, as if the action might ensconce her from pain.

The endeavor was ineffective, and Leonora paced her room.

This was her fault.

How could she have been so foolish as to concoct such an idiotic plan? All that had happened was she'd lost her heart and virginity to Sebastian.

And now she could never be happy.

Her body ached, as if some terrible beast was gnawing on her ribs.

A knock sounded on her door, then her mother entered.

"Mama?" Leonora's eyes widened, and she flinched.

Mama strode into the room, clothed in a night rail and robe that reminded Leonora of the old days, when Mama still lived at home.

Leonora sat abruptly on the bed. Suddenly, the room was far too small.

Her mother sat beside her. "Come here."

Leonora felt herself crumple, and her mother swept her into a hug. Mama patted her head, and for a moment, that was enough.

"Sabrina told me what happened," Mama said.

"She shouldn't have told you."

"She had a feeling I would understand," Mama said. "And she was correct."

Leonora gave a wobbly smile. Perhaps there was a benefit to the fact Mama was not like other mothers. Perhaps other parents might have been horrified by the fact Sabrina had seen Leonora alone with a man. Mama did not give a tirade nor did she scold. Instead, Mama hugged her.

"Now, what's this about a duke trap?" Mama asked.

Oh.

Leonora stiffened.

Mama raised an eyebrow. "Sabrina told me."

"I wanted to prove to the world how dreadful Sebastian was." Nausea crept up the back of Leonora's throat as she said the words, and her cheeks heated. "I thought if Sebastian was caught in a compromising position, he would be tarnished."

Mama gave her a wry smile. "I think you still have some things to learn about society."

Leonora's shoulders slumped. "It was a foolish plan."

"Then I take it you weren't against being caught in a compromising position with him now?"

"I didn't like being caught," Leonora said, "but the actual position…"

"Was thrilling?" Mama giggled, and even though Leonora had never been so unhappy before, she found herself smiling.

After all, being with Sebastian *had* been nice.

"It doesn't matter though." Leonora frowned. "He was very cross. Then he left the castle to go goodness knows where. He'll never forgive me."

"I see," Mama said soberly. She tilted her head. "There's a reason that boy is wary of you."

"I'm sure I can't imagine what it could be. He started everything. He sent that painting to Eloisa as a wedding present."

"It's quite a good painting of me," Mama said.

Leonora crossed her arms. "You're not being helpful."

"I'm trying to be," Mama said. "Your father was not very good to Sebastian and his family."

Leonora raised her eyebrow. "I don't want you to speak poorly of Papa."

"That's admirable. I'm pleased you remember your father with such fondness."

"Then why are you trying to ruin that?" Leonora asked and got up quickly. She strode around the room, and her skirts brushed against the various sideboards, chaise longues, and ottomans strewn about the room in an artistic manner.

"Your father loved you," Mama said, "but he did not love his next-door neighbor."

"Because clearly the Dartmouths are terrible people," Leonora said, though the words hurt her throat as she uttered them.

"Your father tricked the late duke into giving a large portion of his estate to us. In fact, Timothy still has the land."

Leonora looked at her mother. "That can't be true."

"Of course it's true." Mama rose. "It happened at the gaming table. Sebastian's late father was drunk and didn't know he was gambling with the note for much of his farmland. He used to claim your father had deceived him."

"What did Papa say?"

Mama sighed. "He was proud to have won the land."

Leonora wrinkled her brow. "That doesn't make sense. I'm certain Father and the duke were always friends. At least until…"

"They always fought?"

Leonora nodded, but her cheeks warmed, as if she was a schoolchild who'd made a basic error.

"Why do you think Sebastian has been so open in his dislike?" Mama pressed.

Leonora was still for a moment, pondering this. Finally, she frowned. "I'm certain it was merely business."

"Yes," Mama agreed, "it was merely business, but for Sebastian's father, it was personal. He'd considered your father a friend, and he died shortly after. Now, how was a young boy to think about the neighbors who put his father under so much stress during his final days? That's how hatred is formed, my dear."

"Yes," Leonora said softly. Her voice lacked its earlier firmness, and her heart bounced up and down in her chest indecisively. "That was years ago though. Papa has been dead for a long time. What does that have to do with anything now?"

"I hope it doesn't *need* to affect anything now," Mama said, "but it does mean you could perhaps be a bit more understanding."

"After what he's done?" Leonora widened her eyes.

"Yes," Mama said. "Exactly. That's the reason. Do you love him?"

Leonora's heart thundered and thumped and thrummed. Her mouth dried. "I don't know."

Disappointment fluttered over Mama's face, and she drew back. "I suppose it is a difficult question."

Leonora pressed her lips together, but she knew the answer. She sighed. "No, I don't love him."

Mama frowned. "Oh."

Leonora was wondering whether her mother was thinking about all the ways they were different.

"I can't love him," Leonora explained. "It's impossible."

Mama's eyes narrowed. "And why is that, my dear?"

"Because I'm going to marry someone else. Sebastian will be a memory." Leonora lifted her chin, and she knew the statements were true. Loving Sebastian was an absurdity. After all, he'd left. Now the most important thing for her to do was forget him.

"Lord Knightley?" Mama asked.

Leonora frowned.

"You could tell him you changed your mind, that you were nervous. He might understand."

Visions of a life with Lord Knightley flittered through Leonora's mind, and her body tensed. "I already told him no."

"So someone else."

"Or no one else," Leonora said. "I shouldn't assume anyone else will offer. Perhaps I'll be a governess. It doesn't matter. The principle remains the same: I will not spend the rest of my life thinking about him. I will not even spend the rest of the night thinking of him."

"I see."

Leonora rose matter-of-factly. "It's time for me to go to bed."

Mama's eyes twitched, and Leonora had the horrible feeling her display of maturity and sensibleness had not been believable. "You want me to leave?"

Leonora raised her chin. "Indeed."

Mama's face sobered, and she held Leonora's hand in her own. "I'm worried about you."

"I'm absolutely fine. You mustn't worry. Besides, I'm sure Julius is wondering where you are."

Mama averted her gaze.

"You don't think that I don't know that you spend the nights together?" Leonora asked impatiently.

Mama managed to appear chastened.

"I wonder why you're not married."

"I wouldn't have thought you should have anyone to replace your father, given with what force you always exalt his rather questionable merits," Mama said.

"Not all his merits were questionable."

"Perhaps not," Mama agreed. "He did love you. But this isn't a question about me and Julius. This is a question about you and Sebastian. You always were so close when you were little."

"That was a long time ago." Leonora lifted her chin to such a degree that if she'd placed a book on top of it, it would have slid back and clattered to the floor.

"I think you love Sebastian," Mama said. "You're afraid to admit it."

"I'm not afraid of anything." Leonora placed her hands on her waist. "You know that."

"You're afraid of your feelings because they're so large."

Leonora's eyes widened. "You don't know that."

"Oh, but darling, I do," Mama said. "Because I was absolutely the same, and you are not going to make the mistake I did when I married your father."

Leonora narrowed her eyes promptly.

Mama shook her head. "I do not want to discuss your father, but I will tell you we never should have been married. I didn't love him. And I doubt you are going to love the next man. Not like you love Sebastian. The passion between you practically vibrates through the room. It's obvious."

"It doesn't matter what I think," Leonora said softly. "He's not here. He left."

"Then you must fix it. You have to go after him and make him listen to you."

"But that wouldn't be dignified."

"I assure you that leading an unhappy life is not dignified. No one will laud you for that. You must seize your happiness."

Leonora sighed. "Mother, I can't. I wouldn't know what to say."

"Tell him the truth. But don't wait, sweetheart. Life only gives us so many chances. Don't waste yours."

"Is that why you're with Julius?"

Mama nodded. "Yes. Because I love him, and he loves me. I'm determined to clutch happiness, no matter what others say."

With that, Mama kissed Leonora's forehead, then left the room.

Leonora stood still, lost in thought. Her mother's words kept circling.

Drat.

She flung her robe about her, aware she'd already wasted far too much time. She was going to take a chance, even if it was absurd.

Leonora rushed through the corridor, conscious of the late hour. The room was dark and gloomy, but it didn't matter.

Leonora opened the main door, thankful no servant was

placed in the foyer to stare pitying or rebukingly at her.

The crisp wind slammed against her, as if chiding her at having exited the house. She could still change her mind. She could still hurry inside, tuck herself under the covers, and pretend tonight had never happened. After all, Sebastian had used a French sleeve.

She didn't want to live without him. She was certain any life without him would be dull. Perhaps that was why she'd always spent so much time thinking of him. Perhaps they'd both been saddened at being torn apart as children and tried to focus too much on why their fathers despised each other to understand the sudden separation.

It hadn't worked though.

Leonora loved him. There'd only ever been him.

She shut the door gently behind her, anxious not to wake any servants, then hurried along the path. Gravel crunched beneath her feet. The fountain continued to spew, though its water was now inky and the cherubs that played in the pool appeared foreboding.

She made her way to the stables, then opened the large wooden door.

"Who's there?" A servant stared at her. The boy was young. No doubt he worked here.

"I'm sorry," she said.

"I-I didn't expect anyone."

Someone had seen her. Now was the time to make her excuses and flee back to the castle with as much haste as possible. A stable boy seeing her late at night was scandalous, but a stable boy knowing she'd taken a horse to ride off on her own? She shuddered. That was treacherous to everything she'd been taught.

She raised her chin.

Time was vital.

Who knew how far Sebastian had already traveled?

"I'm looking for His Grace," she said.

The stable boy's eyes widened. "He's not here."

"I gathered that." She hesitated. An awkward silence grew between them. "Do you know where he is?"

The stable boy's mouth dropped open.

"It's important. I wouldn't ask if it weren't important."

"I'm not sure if I can share—"

"You must," Leonora said. "The duke will be glad you told me."

"He's going to his estate in Cornwall, miss."

She gave him a wobbly smile. "He's going as far away as he can."

The stable boy blinked.

"Well, I must have a horse."

"I'm not sure whether we have any female saddles."

"I don't need one," Leonora said quickly. "Just prepare it."

The stable boy's eyes widened. "Of course, miss." He scurried away.

"But perhaps you can make certain the horse is gentle?" Leonora despised the pleading in her own voice.

"Bess is very gentle," the stable boy assured her, leading a horse to her.

Unlike other women her age, Leonora had never had a particular fondness for horses. Riding lessons were only slightly more preferable to mathematics and never exceeded the joys of French. She'd certainly never ridden in anything except a normal female saddle.

Still, she was hardly going to ask the stable boy to accompany her on his own horse, and she knew enough about riding to know that it was dangerous for a woman to attempt to disembark from her saddle on her own.

The stable boy assisted her up, and Leonora pretended it was not utterly unladylike for her to ride with her legs splayed over the horse's back. The stable boy averted his eyes, and his cheeks were a decidedly ruddier color than before.

"Thank you," she said.

"That's all right, miss."

She hesitated. "Which way is Cornwall?"

"You'll want to turn right at the end of the drive. I-I don't know which way he'll take to get there."

"Then I'd better catch up with him quickly." With that, Leonora urged her horse into a trot.

Chapter Sixteen

The coach rattled forward, finally leaving the castle behind in the distance. It was a consolation, even if meager. Sebastian leaned against the upholstered seat and pretended he was happy.

His main task now was to forget Leonora. He could do that. He could do anything.

He fluttered his eyes shut, but images of Leonora filled his mind.

Blast.

He opened his eyes hastily and focused on the dim shadows in the carriage.

Horses' hooves sounded, and he turned his head. Who was riding a horse so late at night? And with such determination?

He'd thought he was in the remote countryside, not in Seven Dials.

He drew back the tasseled velvet drapes in his carriage and craned his neck toward the rider.

Then he halted.

Was that Leonora Holt? He shook his head. The thought was impossible.

She wasn't supposed to be here. Not riding by herself. Not here. Not in the middle of the night.

Still. That did look very much like her. Her long hair moved about her in the wind. Heavens, her dress flowed about her, revealing her ankles, her knees, her *thighs*.

He swallowed hard.

She looked seductive.

Blast it.

What was she doing here? She wasn't supposed to ride by herself at this time.

"Halt!" Sebastian banged on the carriage roof, and the driver stopped.

Sebastian scrambled down the metal steps of the carriage. "What on earth are you doing?"

"I wanted to speak with you." Leonora dismounted the horse. She breathed heavily. Sebastian tried to avoid looking at her bosom moving up and down in the moonlight.

"You need to return to your family."

"No." Leonora crossed her arms. Her cheeks were flushed in a delicious manner, and her clothes were unsightly. Mud had evidently splattered over her at some point.

Sebastian's lips twitched, and he forced himself to straighten them.

He was very angry. He mustn't forget that. He mustn't chuckle and sweep her into his arms and smatter kisses all over her adorable nose. She'd tricked him, and he would be a fool to do anything but leave.

"I'm sorry," Sebastian said. "It's too late."

With that, he returned to his carriage and closed the door. He stared firmly in front of him, lest he be swayed by the wild protestations of his heart. Instead, he knocked on the ceiling. "Carry on, Bates."

※

LEONORA STARED AFTER the receding coach as it rumbled along the road. Tears welled in her eyes. That had not gone well. She'd found him, and he'd refused her.

This is the end.

Her chest squeezed as if a boa constrictor was wrapping its way around her. The floral scent emanating from the hedges was too thick, and she tightened her hands around the reins.

The horses, though, continued over the dirt path until the trampling of their hooves lessened and lessened and she couldn't hear them at all.

She frowned. It was late at night, and Sebastian wanted to travel far away. She couldn't catch up with his coach again. She'd been lucky it took her much less time to get ready than it had taken his groom to prepare Sebastian's carriage and get a servant to gather his items.

The horse grunted beneath her, stomping its feet uncertainly.

She inhaled. This was when she turned her horse around. This was when she returned to the stables and informed her mother she'd done the best she could. This was when she started living the life she'd told her mother she would lead, the life that involved forgetting Sebastian.

Blast.

"Let's go." She patted her horse. "We're going after him."

Sebastian had to spend the night somewhere. Perhaps she would find his carriage at the next public house. She raised her chin. She would carry on. She had to.

The horse neighed and continued on the road. The stars sparkled above them, the only things visible here, even though they were impossibly far away.

Leonora's back ached, her hands smarted, and her entire body was cold as the wind swept over it. Still, she kept going.

Finally, after perhaps an hour, a solitary structure appeared in the distance. Leonora pressed forward. Was it an inn? The building was larger than most. It would be unlikely for somebody to place their home so near the road. Carriages were grouped near the building.

Heavens.

It was an inn.

Her heart thrummed, and she urged the horse to quicken its pace. Finally, they reached it. Flower boxes dotted the windows, and a sign dangled from the building: *The Red Rooster.*

Leonora's heart soared, and she surveyed the carriage park.

There in the corner sat the duke's coach. It was unmistakable. It wasn't his nicest coach, of course. The wheels were not painted bright primary colors, and there was no gleaming gold crest hanging from the back, letting everyone know which dukedom he represented.

As carriages went, this was more modest, more discreet, even if it was immaculately maintained. Leonora wouldn't be surprised if he even had a spare carriage wheel somewhere in it, as if the groom had insisted the duke was a man of such importance he couldn't even wait to get a new carriage wheel made like everyone else did.

Leonora moved her head toward the public house. Half-timbered beams crisscrossed its facade, and flowers peaked from flower boxes. No doubt they looked marvelous in the sunshine. Now, though, there were only a few lights to illuminate them, and they cast scraggly shadows over the wall.

She glanced at the door. She suddenly wished she'd had the good sense to dress up as a man like her sister Eloisa had once done. How on earth could she simply saunter into the public house?

She craned her neck, wondering which room Sebastian might be in. If only all his rooms were equipped with trees. Unfortunately, there was not a single one here.

She sighed, tied her horse, then crept inside the public house. A bell rang as she entered, and she stiffened. The sound seemed impossibly loud. The room was large but empty. There were no conversations being held at the round tables dotted about the room. No barmaid marched up and down the aisles, handing tankards to chuckling men. Nobody was playing the piano or violin, and nobody was singing.

Perhaps she could peek at the register. She glanced at the

large bar. Yes, that was what she would do. Her heart swelled once again, and she moved forward, eager to have a plan.

Once she knew which room she was in, she could knock on his door. She could pretend to be a maid perhaps. And then once she was inside…her heart thrummed. Well, then they could speak and she would let him know just how much she loved him.

It was all very simple.

She shouldn't have worried that she hadn't had a plan at all.

She marched to the bar and began searching to find something that resembled a register.

There it was. A book filled with the names of people on one side and rooms on the other. She flipped to the last page.

Unfortunately, at that moment, a rotund woman wearing a white cap and a dark dress that looked like it had been thrown over her hastily came through the door.

This must be the publican, and Leonora smoothed her gown and pretended she hadn't snuck onto this side of the counter.

The publican gave her a strange glance. "What on earth are you doing there? And what are you holding?"

Leonora stiffened and dropped the register.

"Out." The publican pointed. "Now."

Leonora scrambled away from the counter, looking lingeringly at the register.

"Forgive me, I only wanted to ascertain the location of the Duke of Dartmouth's room. I did not desire to wake anyone."

The publican narrowed her eyes. "You only wanted to ascertain the duke's private location?" Sarcasm rippled through the publican's voice. "That's absolutely none of your concern. This is a respectable institution."

Leonora bit her lip. Of course, the publican was correct, but her skin warmed.

The publican kept her eyes narrowed. "Are you by yourself, miss?"

Leonora's heartbeat quickened. She shook her head, even though she'd never been prone to lying. "Of course not."

The publican frowned. "I'm certain I heard only one horse outside."

"I'm traveling in a carriage. It must have sounded like one horse."

"I believe you're lying, young lady. I don't appreciate that. I don't appreciate young ladies coming here and lying to see a duke. We don't want our guests treated that way. What do you intend to do? Force him into a compromising position?"

Leonora widened her eyes. "Naturally not."

The publican's frown deepened. "Or are you a lady of the night? Though, your outfit lacks feathers and fineries." She scowled. "We don't want you inside. Please leave immediately."

Heavens.

Leonora needed to do something. She couldn't be tossed from the inn. She needed to speak with Sebastian.

Otherwise, what would happen?

The publican had called her a lady of the night. It was possible one of the guests would be amenable for some evening excitement and would not listen if she told him she was no such person.

Leonora had been so focused on seeing Sebastian that she'd put herself into this position. She knew better.

Heavens, what would Mrs. Feldman say if she saw her now, wearing just a cloak over her night rail? She would be appalled.

No, there was only one person who could help her.

"Sebastian." She raised her voice and called for him. Unfortunately, no thudding steps sounded and no handsome man appeared in the doorway.

No one had ever said she was very good at shouting. Why would she excel at it now?

Leonora darted her gaze around the public house. She needed to make some noise.

Empty tables were scattered about the room, but something else drew her attention.

A piano.

Leonora hurried toward it.

"What are you doing?" the publican hollered.

Leonora pulled out the piano bench and sat down.

She lifted the lid and placed her hands on the black-and-white keys.

Already she felt more at home.

If she played, perhaps Sebastian would hear her. She knew exactly which song to choose, what Sebastian would recognize.

His song.

The same song she'd played in his music room.

In the next moment, she began to play. She moved her fingers rapidly and forcefully over the keys.

CHAPTER SEVENTEEN

Music drifted through Sebastian's bedroom, and he awoke. Where was he?

But then he remembered. He was at the Red Rooster. Not his own bedroom. Not his own home. He was in a damned public house.

What was that sound? That was *his* music. Was he imagining it? He must be. Yet the melody continued.

He raised his torso. Why would somebody be playing his music now? He blinked into the dark room.

It was piano music though. It must be coming from the public house's dining area.

He rubbed his eyes. Who even knew this song? Somebody who had heard it in London and for some absurd reason had decided to play it when the whole public house was silent? Was it Leonora? Had she continued to follow him?

Was there a chance she was alone in a public house?

Mighty Poseidon.

Leonora must be here. She must have followed him even after he'd explicitly told her not to do so. And now she was downstairs. By herself. And—

Sebastian leaped from his bed and flung his attire on. Leonora wasn't supposed to be here. Women didn't visit public houses alone late at night, and if they did, they certainly weren't supposed to wake up all the guests. She could be in danger.

Sebastian scrambled toward the door. He'd never wandered the halls of a public house, looking so disheveled, but it didn't matter. He just needed to go downstairs.

He scurried over the floorboards. They squeaked beneath his thuds, and he narrowly averted walking into a wall. Finally, he found the staircase and hurried down the steps.

He needed to be there quickly. He needed to find Leonora. Was it her? Was it truly her? The music, though, continued to play.

Finally, he entered the ground floor. Light danced from candles, casting long shadows over the mostly empty room.

The stout proprietress's previous placid features were drawn into a glower. Her hands were on her hips, and her face had taken on a distinctly unnatural red color, the shade not even explained by the shadows in the room. She was directing her attention to the piano player, and Sebastian's heart leaped when he spotted the waifish figure at the keys.

Leonora.

"I demand you stop." The proprietress glared at Leonora, but Leonora continued to play. She focused on the keys, and his heart swelled.

Another door swung wide open, and a man stumbled out. He was clothed in a nightshirt, and his hair, whatever he had left of it, was hidden in a long cap. "What's going on here, Mrs. Bobkins?"

"This lady of the night barged in here asking for the duke," the woman said.

"A lady of the night?" The man's eyes goggled. "In our hamlet? In our pub?"

"Indeed, Mr. Bobkins." The publican's eyes flashed, then she noticed Sebastian's presence, and her hands trembled. "I'm so sorry, Your Grace. I didn't mean for you to be disturbed at all."

The proprietress shot a stern glance at Leonora, who stopped playing the piano.

"This is a travesty." The man clenched his fists and paced the room. "An abomination. In all the centuries of the Red Rooster, I have never heard of anything so despicable happening. To have a woman like you sneaking into our establishment after hours to interrupt a duke's sleep." He shook his head as if to give a silent prayer to his ancestors.

"Don't worry, Your Grace," the proprietress said. "You must go back to bed. We will handle this, and don't worry. We'll be certain to not charge you anything."

"What?" her husband barked.

The proprietress gave her husband a stern look, then he swallowed hard, his Adam's apple easily visible now that his neck was no longer covered by a necktie. "Er—yes. Naturally, Your Grace. We will remove the charge."

"That is not necessary," Sebastian said, still staring at Leonora.

She looked so slender, and her eyes were wide with obvious fright. And yet she'd come here even when he'd told her not to. He should at least speak with her.

"I will handle this situation myself." He turned to the couple. "You can leave."

"Are you certain, Your Grace?" the proprietress asked. "My husband excels at throwing people out. He's quite strong. He's had a lot of ale, of course, so you don't see his muscles, but all the same, I assure you he is completely capable of picking her up and tossing her from our lovely establishment."

"No one will do that," Sebastian said, then his eyes narrowed. "Except perhaps me."

"Very well, Your Grace." The couple scurried away. Their footsteps pounded over the floorboards, and when the door closed, Sebastian approached Leonora.

Her hair cascaded over her shoulders, and her clothes were creased. Unfortunately, neither fact hampered her beauty, and Sebastian forced himself to steel his emotions.

"What are you doing here?" Sebastian asked sternly.

"I came to see you," Leonora said.

His lips twitched despite himself. "You mean you didn't just come to make use of the piano here?"

She shook her head, and for a moment, her lips swerved up.

Then Sebastian remembered all the reasons nothing could possibly be normal between them. Leonora had tricked him. She'd laid a trap for him. Nothing with her was real.

"I already told you to go home," he growled.

"But I didn't listen."

"No," Sebastian agreed.

"I didn't listen," Leonora said, rising from her seat, "because I care for you."

She strolled closer to him, and her scent wafted about him in a most distracting manner. "I know it's not proper for me to do this, but it was important for me to tell you everything."

"I see." His voice was hoarse. He thought he might actually understand, but he was worried he was only seeing what he wanted to believe.

"It's true," she said, as if reading his mind. Then she took his hands. Hers were cold, and he was reminded of the fact she had actually traveled on horseback after his coach. He wrapped his hands over hers, wanting to warm them. Energy surged through him, spurred by the very touch with her, and his heartbeat quickened.

"I can't believe you're here," he said finally.

"Of course I'm here."

"Now. What did you have to tell me so urgently?"

She hesitated, then she jutted up her chin in a brave manner. "I love you. I should have said so before, but I was frightened."

Sebastian blinked and drew back.

Whatever he'd anticipated, it wasn't that. He'd expected an apology.

But that...

He swallowed hard, noting with irritation that his heart was fluttering, even though it shouldn't.

"You don't—"

"I do," Leonora said. "I'm so incredibly sorry."

"Oh." Sebastian stared at her, still uncertain.

"I've never said that to anyone before."

"I hadn't either," Sebastian said, his voice husky as he remembered the pain of earlier tonight.

"You've always been the only person on my mind," Leonora told him. "There's never been anyone else. Maybe even from when we were little and separated in such a manner. I'm so sorry, but I care for you immensely. You must know that. As for the plan, that was foolish and childish."

This was when Sebastian was supposed to tell her that no apology could ever suffice. This was when he sent her away, for the final time.

But something made him hesitate.

She made him hesitate.

⇶⇷

SHE'D SAID IT. She'd said everything.

Her heart clenched. The words seemed so feeble.

Was this when he would arch his eyebrow? When he would shoot her a boyish grin that landed at her heart with the effectiveness of the most skilled archer?

Was this when he chided her again for wasting his time? Or worse, explained that what had happened between them meant nothing and that she was a foolish little girl to imagine otherwise?

There'd been a reason her first instinct had been to do nothing, so that she might emanate some sophistication.

Now wasn't the time for sophistication though. It was the time to bear her soul. This was her only opportunity.

"I think I've always loved you," she said. "That's why I was so angry when I learned about your family. I-I didn't know what my father had done."

"You didn't?" His eyes widened.

She shook her head silently. "Mama explained it to me tonight. I feel terrible."

"I see." He shifted his weight from leg to leg.

Heavens.

He was going to tell her to leave. She resisted the temptation to shut her eyes.

"I'm sorry," he said finally.

She jerked her head into a nod.

"I do care for you." He frowned. "Perhaps I should have faith. I'm tired of abhorring you."

"I am too."

"I suppose I have not always behaved in an ideal fashion," he mused.

She gave him a wobbly smile.

"Perhaps we can forget about my terrible taste in gifts and your dreadful duke trap."

She nodded frantically. "I'd like that."

"Good." His eye shimmered. "After all, I still love you."

Leonora stared at him.

Had she imagined those words? Her heart sang.

"What now?" Leonora asked quietly.

"Now we kiss."

"Is that all we do?"

Sebastian chuckled. The warm amber sound of his voice filled the room, and Leonora's worry dissipated.

"No," Sebastian promised.

He dragged her to him and began to kiss her.

This time, there was no hesitation, no shyness.

This time, Leonora knew she was kissing the man who loved her. Happiness surged through her.

Sebastian continued to kiss her. His lips claimed her skin.

"I still think it's important to talk about everything." He lifted her into his arms.

"Oh, precisely," she murmured between kisses.

Sebastian marched her up the stairs, clutching her in his arms.

She nestled against his sturdy chest. Finally, he opened the door to a room and carried her to a large bed.

"We can confer here," Sebastian declared.

"An intimate conference."

"Quite right." He whispered into her ear, "very intimate."

Butterflies fluttered through Leonora's body, as if attempting to play a symphony.

Sebastian withdrew, then returned with candles. "I hope you know I'm going to marry you."

Happiness surged through Leonora. "You are?"

"Indeed," he said lightly. "Unless you mind?"

"I don't," she said quickly, and he grinned.

Sebastian lay on the bed and pulled her into his arms. He moved his hands over her figure, and his cotton scent wafted about her. His hands found her rounded bosom, and he moved them over her globes.

He pressed his lips to the nape of her neck and tasted her skin.

"You found me," he murmured.

"I did." Leonora's voice shook, and he tucked his fingers into the bodice of her gown, freeing her bosom. He trailed his fingers over her soft skin, and her peaks tightened and pebbled beneath his touch.

He ran his fingers through her silky strands.

"We're going to have children with red hair," he said.

She laughed. "There is a high chance." She hesitated. "Do you mind?"

"Of course not." This time, he chuckled, and he pulled her closer to him. "I want that. I want to be reminded of you always."

"But my father—"

"Was your father," he said. "I shouldn't have held him against you. I'm sorry."

"And I'm sorry he hurt your family."

"I know."

Sebastian wrapped his arms more tightly around Leonora. She was his.

Sebastian pulled Leonora's night rail over her head. "One layer of clothing is quite enough."

"How revolutionary," Leonora said wryly.

"Intelligent," Sebastian corrected.

"We *are* having a wonderful conference," Leonora said.

"I know." Sebastian smirked.

Then Sebastian captured Leonora's mouth in his, and they were very quiet. Their hands, though, continued to move. As did his cock.

And soon he was once again delving inside of her. This time, she lay down, splayed before him. Her red hair was spread about her shoulders. He was certain he'd never seen a more beautiful sight in his life, and happiness moved through him as they moaned together.

Chapter Eighteen

THE NEXT MORNING, Sebastian awoke with sunlight streaming through the window. He'd always been particularly fond of sunshine, but another, even more blissful sight, met his eye: Leonora.

She lay beside him, her arms wrapped about his torso and her beautiful red hair cascading about her.

He kissed her forehead, and she opened her eyes and blinked.

"Good morning, my love," he murmured.

She gave him a lazy grin. "Good morning, sweetheart."

Then there was much kissing. Finally, he pulled himself away from her succulent, soft lips. "Let's return to the castle."

Her eyes sparkled.

"And then—" He swallowed hard and took her lovely hands in his. "And then I thought we could go to Gretna Green."

A smile played on her beautiful pink lips.

"If you want. Or we could go to Guernsey. Or just stay here, of course."

"I think you would like to elope."

"I want us to marry," he said. "And I don't want to wait." He leaned closer to her. "I don't think your family will permit us to sleep in the same bed otherwise."

"That's a good assessment." She wrapped her arms about him. "And I would very much like to elope. I've always wanted to visit Scotland."

"We can spend the beginning of our married life touring the Highlands," Sebastian said.

Leonora's eyes glimmered. "I have the impression that married life with you will be very wonderful indeed."

"Only because you'll be by my side, my love." Sebastian helped her up. "Let's return. We have an announcement to make."

"You're going to shock Timothy."

"We'll see if my china makes its way through breakfast."

She laughed, and his heart swelled.

Life couldn't be more wonderful. It was a viewpoint he hadn't subscribed to when he'd arrived at the Red Rooster, but now it seemed impossible to ever see the world in any other light.

Bates stood before the carriage.

"Good morning!" Sebastian said cheerfully. "Lovely day, isn't it?"

His driver's eyes rounded and focused on Leonora. Evidently he had not heard the piano music last night or realized its significance.

"Your Grace." Bates bowed, then hesitated and inclined his head. "Miss Holt."

Leonora smiled.

"She won't be Miss Holt for long," Sebastian said.

"Indeed, Your Grace?"

"You'll be able to call her Your Grace soon."

"Ah. Well, that will keep things convenient."

"I thought so."

"Then let me offer you my congratulations."

Sebastian beamed at his driver.

"Do you still want to return to your estate?" Bates asked tactfully.

"We better return to the castle," Sebastian said. "Having a missing sister is something the Holt family might worry about."

"Very astute of you."

"And then we really should give the servants a chance to appropriately pack. Trips to Gretna Green are lengthy."

"Ah. Quite right." Bates smiled, then opened the door to the carriage.

Sebastian followed Leonora inside, and Bates hooked Leonora's horse to the carriage and rode back to the castle.

The coach sped past meadows and sloping fields. Wildflowers jutted their purple-and-pink heads through the long grass for admiration, and everything was beautiful.

"They're going to be surprised to see us," Leonora told him.

"Yes," Sebastian said agreeably. His betrothed was quite wise. She must be the very wisest woman in the world. He was certain in this, as in so many other things, she was absolutely correct.

Finally, Bates stopped in front of the castle, and Sebastian assisted Leonora from the carriage. They strode toward the entrance, and Sebastian knocked on the door.

The butler opened the door, and his eyes goggled. "It's you?"

"Indeed." Sebastian stepped inside and gestured to Leonora. "And this is my betrothed."

Something clattered, and Sebastian realized the butler had dropped something.

"Forgive me, Your Grace, I was surprised."

"No matter." Sebastian strolled over the glossy black-and-white tiles in the foyer. "Where is everyone?"

"The breakfast room, Your Grace."

Sebastian grinned. "Come, my love."

He took Leonora's hand and sauntered with her to the breakfast room.

He waited for surprise to form on everyone's faces, but instead they continued to sip their coffee and chew on their toast.

"Ah! Leonora." Timothy beamed. "You already went on a walk?"

"No." Leonora strode closer. "We didn't."

"They were out all night," Mrs. Holt declared with a pleased smile on her face.

The room was suddenly silent. Apparently toast had lost its attraction, despite the abundance of marmalade and jam.

Timothy shot Mrs. Holt a stern glance. "Do you mean to tell me you knew that dearest Leonora was outside?"

"Indeed." A smug smile flickered over her face.

"That explains why Lord Knightley left early," Timothy muttered.

Sebastian winked at Leonora's mother, and Mrs. Holt swallowed back a chuckle.

"Are you fine?" Constance said with a worried expression on her face, glancing at Leonora as if trying to determine whether she'd sprained her ankle, broken a leg, or had any other indication that she had an excuse for being absent.

But Leonora looked marvelous. She always looked marvelous, after all.

Though, Sebastian had to admit that normally her dress was rather smoother than it was at its current moment. Perhaps Sebastian needed to practice removing her dress, and shift, and stays and tossing them on the opposite side of the carriage rather more.

He smiled. He didn't mind practicing that at all.

"You look happy," Eloisa said with an odd expression on her face. She moved her gaze to Sebastian, and her eyes were wide, though she said nothing.

Sebastian sighed. He was afraid he'd scared Eloisa on occasion before. He hadn't been fond of the idea that she'd wanted to remove paintings of Mrs. Holt, and she'd known the full extent of his displeasure.

Sabrina also looked at him warily. He sighed again. He'd been, no doubt, unappealing to her as a prospective brother-in-law. Still, that had been in the past. Now it was the start of his future.

"I must apologize to you both," he told Eloisa and Sabrina. "I have behaved in a most dastardly fashion. I pray one day you can forgive me."

They nodded.

"Now we have something to announce," Sebastian said and took Leonora's hand in his. Even though this was hardly the first time, even this morning, that they'd held hands, a jolt of energy surged through him.

Timothy's mouth dropped open, and he raked his hand through his pale-red hair in a befuddled manner before shooting a glance to his wife as if to assure himself he was not completely losing his senses. Certainly his wife seemed to understand his unspoken plea, for she nodded to him softly.

"Is it a good announcement?" Sabrina asked tentatively.

Mrs. Holt's eyes shimmered. "I'm certain it's a good announcement."

Julius looked at her. "I have the impression you know something."

"Well." Mrs. Holt sighed. "A mother does have her instincts."

"I see." Julius stared at Sebastian and Leonora, then he moved his eyes to their joined hands. He raised an eyebrow in a languid fashion. "Judging from the position of their limbs and the fact they are currently entwined, I would venture a hypothesis that they are about to announce their affection for each other."

Glass shattered, and Timothy had a very red look on his face. A maid darted toward him, colliding with a chair before she quickly hurried to his side and began to dab up the spilled coffee that had fallen from the broken porcelain.

"We're going to get married." Sebastian's heart expanded again just at the mere words.

From the shocked looks on everyone else's faces, it was possible that their hearts were also expanding. Why else would their eyebrows be thrust to the very top of their foreheads? And why else would they be clutching their heads as if their hair might fall off?

"Are you jesting?" Eloisa asked.

"No," Leonora declared.

"Of course she's not joking," Sabrina scolded her sister.

"Leonora isn't prone to being humorous." Eloisa nodded, and Leonora knitted her brows in obvious frustration.

"You're humorous enough for me, my love," Sebastian assured his bride-to-be.

"I doubt he's very humorous either." Sabrina crossed her arms and gave him a fixed, assessing stare as if pondering his qualities as a potential addition to the family.

From the firm glance she gave him, he had the distinct impression she was not overly pleased at the prospect.

Sebastian sighed. "As I said before, I apologize. I'm afraid I haven't always been on my best behavior."

Eloisa snorted, and Timothy shook his head at her in a disapproving fashion.

"In fact, my behavior was terrible. Utterly reprehensible. But please know I love your sister very much and will do everything I can to be a good husband to her and a good brother-in-law to both of you."

Eloisa's and Sabrina's faces softened, but Timothy's expression remained stern.

"He must have harmed her," Timothy said, and his face whitened, which had the odd effect of making his freckles stand out even more.

Damnation.

"Dartmouth," Timothy growled, and he left his seat with a force that made Sebastian regret he'd ever considered Timothy to be lacking in athleticism.

"Sit down," Constance said in a quiet voice. She tugged on her husband's sleeve.

Timothy only tightened his fists together as if he desired to pummel Sebastian to bits.

"That's not the ideal reaction," Sebastian said dryly.

"You think I don't know what you must have done?" Timothy asked. "It's obvious. You must think there's a baby on the way."

"Darling…," Constance said, "Don't you think that if there's a baby on the way, even potentially, that it's best if you not batter him?"

"No." Timothy thumped his hand on the table. "No, I'm not letting my beloved sister be attached to such a despicable character. We'll find a solution. We'll go to Switzerland. You can tell everyone the child is Constance's and mine. We'll raise him or her like our own."

"We will not go to Switzerland," Leonora said. "I assure you I am quite happy about this."

"Well." Timothy bit his lip. "I suppose you will be a duchess."

"That's not why I'm happy."

Timothy eyed Sebastian skeptically. "Are you saying there are other advantages to marrying him?"

"Of course there are," Leonora reassured him.

"That's quite a charitable instinct," Constance said approvingly. "The vicar would be most proud of you."

"I don't think my thoughts about Sebastian would be quite appropriate for him," Leonora said, and then her face pinkened in a most adorable way.

Heavens, Sebastian was marrying a goddess.

"We love each other," Sebastian repeated.

Timothy's eyes goggled.

"That's terribly romantic of you and quite suitable," Mama said.

Cornelius's jaw fell. "But you despise each other."

"No," Sebastian said. "That was in the past. I've made a point to no longer do that. Not the best way to start a marriage, don't you think?"

"Yes, it is optimal not to detest the person you're marrying," Cornelius said slowly. "I do agree in that, but I'm just confused. Was there something in your will saying you needed to marry before the age of thirty?"

"Of course not," Sebastian said. "My father would never have made such an atrocious will."

"Then why her? I mean, I know there aren't many people in

the countryside. If you had the sudden urge to marry, London is filled with young ladies and you are quite eligible."

"Not anymore," Sebastian reminded him. "After all, I'm to be married."

"But you've always been a marriage opposer." Cornelius gaped.

"That, my dear friend, was in the past. Now I'm in the future and I am very much a marriage proponent, I assure you," Sebastian said.

Cornelius goggled. "Very well. Splendid. Well, I mean, that makes everything convenient. No awkward house parties." Cornelius tilted his head. "I assume you intend to have a happy marriage. Shouting couples can be most awkward."

"I am not going to shout at Leonora," Sebastian said. "She is an angel, a goddess, my true mate." Then he gave a fond smile. "I think she always was."

Cornelius's eyes widened, and he looked at Percival.

"Good God," Percival said, "I think you truly mean it."

"That explains why he never wanted to marry," Cornelius said.

Sebastian nodded, and then a wide smile filled Percival's face.

"I say, I am quite happy for you," Percival said.

Timothy nodded warily. He sat back down, though Sebastian noticed he did not pick up his coffee, as if he'd learned from his earlier mishap and was unwilling to shatter more Staffordshire china.

Leonora smiled up at Sebastian, and his heart swelled.

"We would like to go to Gretna Green," Sebastian said.

"You mean to elope?" Timothy's eyes widened further, even though Sebastian had not thought that feat possible.

"Few people visit Gretna Green for sightseeing," Sebastian said. "And I do not mean to be the exception."

"But surely you want a larger wedding," Constance said.

Sebastian shook his head, still embarrassed at the inappropriate gift he'd given Eloisa and her husband.

Timothy's eyebrows furrowed. "Is there a *chance* there's a child?"

Timothy swallowed hard, evidently unsure whether he could say more. He shot concerned looks at both Sabrina and Leonora.

Sebastian didn't know for certain, but he suspected Percival and Sabrina had already had carnal relations, despite their still unmarried state. And as for Leonora and him, well, he was quite sure there was nothing Timothy could say that would shock her.

"That's not why we want to go to Gretna Green," Sebastian said. "But I am not anxious to wait for our marriage and our wedded life to start."

"So you truly don't desire a large ceremony?"

"No." Sebastian chewed on his lip. "Though, I thought we could all go together."

Leonora jerked her head toward him and beamed. "Truly?"

"I want your family to be there."

"My darling," she breathed.

He turned to the others. "The weather is good now. I think the travel might be enjoyable."

"You could get a special license with your position," Timothy said. "You could marry here."

Sebastian shook his head. "And wait for word to get to Canterbury? No, I'd rather not do that.

"Unless"—he turned to Leonora—"you would. I could throw you the largest wedding imaginable, something to rival Princess Charlotte's."

"That's not necessary," Leonora said. "A trip to Gretna Green sounds lovely. I am certain Scotland is pretty this time of year."

"Then it's settled," Sebastian said, and he kissed her right there in front of everyone.

Epilogue

Three months later

A FLORAL SCENT invaded his nostrils, and Sebastian wedged between two women who were obviously fond of French perfume.

"Another Holt wedding," one woman said.

"I do like their wedding gowns," the other woman said. "Such creativity."

Finally, the music began.

Sebastian waved to Leonora as she strolled down the aisle after Sabrina. "That's my wife," he said to the women beside him.

"You've mentioned that before, Your Grace."

"But she's beautiful, isn't she?" Sebastian declared. "She's the most wonderful woman imaginable."

If he didn't know better, he would've thought the women beside him were rolling their eyes. Naturally, they wouldn't do that. How could anyone not agree with him?

He gazed at Leonora. She was clad in white, in a dress that Sabrina had designed, as she stood beside both her sisters. The organist was playing as they marched down the aisle, where Percival stood, waiting for the ceremony to begin.

Percival moved his legs from side to side as if that might hasten the rest of the ceremony. Sebastian's lips twitched. He had definitely made the right decision to go straight to Gretna Green with Leonora. He didn't know how Percival had managed to wait till the end of the summer, even if Sebastian did have to agree that everyone's attire looked wonderful. He'd heard from Leonora that Sabrina had already had some orders from other people in the home to create dresses for them. He had no doubt in his mind that more orders would be coming after this wedding.

The bishop raised his eyebrows when he saw Sabrina.

Sabrina had the same red hair as her sister Eloisa. It was rare to see so many redheads at once. A surge of pride went through Sebastian that he had married one of the Holt sisters.

The rest of his life would be very exciting. Leonora was now living with him in his large, normally empty town house. The house was filled with her piano music, and Sebastian had never composed so much before, as he was often scribbling, in the library, all the music that was in his mind and heart.

Finally, the bishop married Percival and Sabrina, and everyone clapped. The newly married couple marched down the aisle, and Sebastian scurried up from his pew to meet Leonora. He swept her into a kiss, and she chuckled.

"You're not supposed to do that," Leonora scolded him.

Sebastian shrugged nonchalantly. "We're married now. I'm enjoying my title."

"You're going to be known as the eccentric duke."

"Perhaps." Sebastian tilted his head. "Though, to tell the truth, I don't think I would mind. I don't think I much care what people think of me now."

"Oh." She widened her eyes. "Does that mean—"

"I'm going to tell people at Covent Garden to just use my name at the next opera. I don't want to keep secrets anymore."

She beamed. "How lovely."

Even though Leonora was always just a bit more proper than he was, she gave him a kiss right there and then.

His heart swelled with joy, and he took her hand as they walked toward Timothy's town house for the wedding breakfast.

Today wasn't a pleasant day. The sky was gray, and rain drizzled down. But with Leonora beside him, Sebastian was certain he couldn't imagine anything more wonderful.

"Wasn't it a delightful ceremony?" Mrs. Holt clapped her hands, then she gave Sebastian a stern look. "You could have done the same."

"I know. But I was married to Leonora a few months longer. What could possibly be nicer than that?"

"Oh, you are a charming man." She turned to Leonora. "My dear darling, you did marry an enchanting man, so utterly funny." She waved a fan above her face. Something glimmered from her ring finger.

Sebastian tilted his head. "That's a very lovely ring, Mrs. Holt."

"It is, isn't it?" Mrs. Holt's eyes glimmered, and she held it up to him. "It's a ruby. Julius gave it to me. It goes with my hair."

"It certainly does," Sebastian said. "And for what occasion did he give it to you?"

Mrs. Holt giggled. "I think you've already guessed."

"Well, then, let me extend my deepest congratulations. I'm very happy for you."

She smiled. "I'm enjoying being happy."

He nodded. "I am as well."

And he always would.

Finally, they reached Timothy's town house. Timothy no longer glowered when Sebastian entered, and Constance no longer darted nervous looks, as if contemplating the likelihood that Sebastian would set fire to the place.

Leonora settled at the piano. He slid beside her on the bench, and she smiled. His darling wife moved her fingers with such expertise over the keys. His heart danced along with the merry rhythm of the music, surging in the same happy, fast tempo.

What would have happened if they'd avoided each other like polite acquaintances?

"I'm glad you tried to trap me," he admitted.

She giggled. "We're going to have a very happy ending."

About the Author

Born in Texas, Bianca Blythe spent four years in England. She worked in a fifteenth-century castle, though sadly that didn't actually involve spotting dukes and earls strutting about in Hessians.

She credits British weather for forcing her into a library, where she discovered her first Julia Quinn novel. She remains deeply grateful for blustery downpours.

After meeting her husband in another library, she moved with him to sunny California, though on occasion she still dreams of the English seaside, scones with clotted cream, and sheep-filled pastures. For now, she visits them in her books.

facebook.com/groups/biancablythereaders
instagram.com/biancablytheauthor
biancablythe.com

CPSIA information can be obtained
at www.ICGtesting.com
Printed in the USA
BVHW091337060522
636308BV00014B/770